Nate Bantry was his name.

He said he was her boss, a vintner, and now her legal custodian.

He called her "Cammy." "Cammy Corwin," short for Cameo. A strange name, she thought. But she couldn't remember. She was a victim of amnesia. Her only memory was fear. And she had questions. Who was she . . . and what was her real relationship to Nate Bantry?

Why would an employer take such a personal and expensive interest in a mere secretary? What was Nate Bantry's stake in her past that he so tenaciously clung to her future?

The
Secret of the
Vineyard

Monica Heath

A SIGNET BOOK

Published by
THE NEW AMERICAN LIBRARY
OF CANADA LIMITED

Copyright © 1968 by Monica Heath

First Printing, November, 1968

SIGNET TRADEMARK REG. U.S. PAT. OFF. AND FOREIGN COUNTRIES
REGISTERED TRADEMARK — MARCA REGISTRADA
HECHO EN WINNIPEG, CANADA

SIGNET BOOKS are published in Canada by
The New American Library of Canada Limited
Toronto, Ontario

PRINTED IN CANADA

COVER PRINTED IN U.S.A.

Chapter One

There are times even yet when I must pinch myself in order to believe that any of it is real—the stone winery set into the hillside above this towering, old house and the vines spreading away over the steep, gravelly slopes. Rieslings. The austere Pinots. Sauvignon Blanc. And most particularly the Zinfandels, ragged now, the last of their bronzed leaves falling to blanket the brown earth.

It was because the musically zigzagging name of that particular grape had somehow remained firmly fixed in my mind that I first came to Vinecroft, a victim of amnesia, without the least idea of what my rightful name might be. Now that I am certain once more who I am I feel compelled to capture the incredible events of the past few weeks on paper in an effort to render them believable.

The logical place to begin my story seems to be

with the frightening "accident" that robbed me of memory, leaving me exposed and vulnerable to the whims of a man who seemed to have lost all contact with reason.

I had seen the car before, I was certain of it. It seemed unbelievable that the man inside might have followed me all of the way to San Francisco. Yet some chilling instinct told me that he had and a feeling of panic crept over me. Did he know that I was alone in the city, one of hundreds of girls who converged on the noisy town every week searching for excitement and glamour? Or, like myself, merely hoping to blot out some unbearable tragedy? At that particular thought, my hand rose unconsciously to caress the cameo brooch pinned to my collar.

I was dressed to go out, had planned to find some quiet place for dinner. But the presence of the black car—a Mercedes of uncertain vintage—intimidated me and I turned from the window and began to unpack instead, hanging my clothes carefully in the musty closet. If the car didn't leave soon, I told myself, I would mention its presence to Mrs. Talbot, the crippled woman who lived in the other half of the outdated duplex that I had been fortunate enough to find my first day in town.

As I moved between bags and closet I became aware of the sound of a car's engine and hurried to the window in time to see the car pull out from the curb and roll slowly away. I was able to tell myself then that the presence of the Mercedes had been a coincidence, that I had been foolish to imagine that the man whose face was no more than a pale blur behind the wheel had some evil design on me.

Slipping into my coat, I ventured bravely out into the cool, moist evening. Mrs. Talbot had told me earlier that the North Beach district was only a few blocks distant and I set off in that general direction, longing suddenly for the earthy warmth and gusto characteristic of the Italian people.

I had gone perhaps three blocks when I realized that the car had returned and was following me at a discreet distance. Its low-throated growl rose above the other street sounds in sharp, angry bursts, sending a chill through me. I increased my pace, my heart suddenly a trip-hammer as I hurried past a church with quaint, gothic-patterned doors and, incongruously, a butcher shop where whole carcasses moved through broad doors on an overhead rack to dangle above sawdust floors.

Coming to a corner I turned abruptly, all but running now past delicatessens and a sausage company that cast a zesty redolence into the street. A café sign dangled ahead of me and I pushed frantically through dingy, swinging doors into a low-ceilinged room festooned with artificial grapevines. Cowering briefly against the smoky panes I watched the dark car glide by on a single, vicious roar to disappear into the line of traffic beyond my view.

Only then did I dare to slip into one of the shadowy booths, thinking that I had somehow managed to evade the mysterious man behind the wheel. A plump, moustached waitress appeared, her white blouse immaculate, her black skirt straining around cumbersome hips, and I tried to lose myself in the unfamiliar entrées of the menu she handed me, wishing fervently that I hadn't come to San Francisco, that I'd had more courage.

Capellini. Green tagliarini. Squab. I ordered recklessly, then realized that I wasn't hungry and wondered why I had bothered. I felt suddenly depressed by the robust voices around me, the uninhibited conversation and peals of laughter. For all of their waxy imperfection, the plastic vines twining over the low ceiling reminded me of the Zinfandels that had mantled the courtyard of the Spanish stucco house that had until now been my home, and my throat tightened. A strangling sensation came over me and I paid my bill quickly and darted out once more into the zesty night.

There was no sign of the car and I began to run, the tears that had burned behind my eyelids flowing freely now, blinding me. Ahead of me a tower loomed and I realized that I had arrived unexpectedly at the base of Telegraph Hill. Rickety stairs climbed upward on my right, zigzagging between flat-roofed apartment houses. I paused at its base, becoming chillingly aware once more of the unmistakable hum of the black car. Panic seized me with sudden force and I dashed heedlessly upward, my shoes clattering over the loose, weathered boards. The sound came nearer, and glancing back over my shoulder I glimpsed the Mercedes coming into view, prowling slowly along the street below.

The stairs ended abruptly at the foot of a steep, winding path and I pushed my way recklessly into tangled growth, pausing behind a prickly, low-growing evergreen to listen. Somewhere to my right the car revved savagely. Then the sound faded into the bedlam of the city and was lost. I fancied that the man behind the wheel had cut the motor and was waiting somewhere below for me to reappear on the clambering stairs, and I thought craftily that I would finish my climb to the top of the hill and take another route down. There would be cars at the top, I told myself reassuringly. People. At least for a little while I would be safe.

I scrambled upward only to find the large, macadam lot at the base of the tower dismayingly empty. I realized then that the tower was closed at this hour of the day and that I was alone.

A chilling wariness came over me and I stood poised above the city, paralyzingly aware of my isolation from the blinking, darting, scattering lights below. Sounds rose on the heavy, evening

9

air like the wheezing of some huge writhing beast, in eolithic struggle.

Then suddenly another sound grazed my senses, this one close by, the stertorous murmur of a man's voice repeating my name. I spun disbelievingly and saw a dark form half-hidden in the deep shadows at the base of the tower.

"Who are you?" I cried. "What do you want?"

The dark figure emitted a harsh laugh. A madman, I thought.

Terror swept over me. I glimpsed a hard-surfaced drive spiraling downward on my left and bolted onto it past the Mercedes parked stealthily out of sight beyond the first turn. A thick wall of low-growing evergreens bordered the drive, casting ominous shadows over me as I plunged between them, my only thought to escape that threatening, dark presence that had, for some unbelievable reason, followed me all of the way from Cholami City. There could be no doubt in my mind now that he was the same shadowy-visaged man I had seen spying on the house. I had been alone then, as now, numbed by tragedy, not knowing which way to turn. In the end I had run away. And *he* had followed. Whoever he was, he was stalking me.

Behind me a car door slammed and I heard the Mercedes come raging after me, its tires screaming around the curves. What did he want of me, I wondered frantically. And glanced back to see the chrome nose charging. Heedlessly, I threw myself

10

into the cruelly matted growth, feeling the resilient limbs reject the weight of my body, flinging me backward into the car's careening path.

For a stark, horror-filled instant the gleaming grill leered over me. I knew then that I was going to die and I lay inflamed by a terrifying sense of wonder that there was someone left in the world who cared enough to kill me.

The next moment there was a thud, a shattering explosion inside my head as if the world had fallen on me. Molten pain. Then, mercifully, oblivion.

I fought my way upward out of a fathomless, gray void to see sunlight spilling benignly through French doors. An umbrella table stood beyond the gleaming glass surrounded by gaily striped chairs, and there were young trees espaliered against creamy walls beyond a white-pebbled path that wound beneath naked trellises.

Courtyard. The word came to me out of the wisps of fog that enveloped my mind and I formed it with my lips, turning it into a senseless sound.

"You've decided to come back to us," someone said, reaching to take my hand.

I turned my head and saw a man seated beside my bed. He was smiling, his teeth gleaming out of a face baked a healthy shade of brown.

"Who are you?" I asked in a startled whisper.

"Nate. Nathan Bantry." His smile deepened companionably.

The name meant nothing. His face was the face of a stranger. Only his hand, which was firm and calloused, seemed somehow familiar. I clung to it, trying to remember. But something had drawn a curtain across my mind and there was only an unyielding grayness. It occurred to me that I hadn't the least idea who I was.

"It's gone. Everything is gone," I said in that same frightened whisper. "I can't re . . . rember."

"Remember," the man corrected me kindly. "Don't try, Cammy."

"Cammy?"

"That's you, darling." he said.

"But surely I should remember," I said senselessly.

"Don't worry about it." His eyes that were a translucent shade of brown commanded me. "Just come back to us and stay. That will do nicely for a start. You've been away a long while."

Where, I wondered. Where had I been, I wanted to ask. But the gray mist was gathering around me and I allowed myself to sink into it, drifting sleepily on the gentle tide of his voice.

I suppose days passed, although I have no recollection of time. Vaguely I was aware of Nate Bantry's occasional presence, the sound of his voice speaking to me in comforting tones. And there were others, the ones who had always been there and who, unlike Nate, insisted that I concentrate.

One of them appeared now, a platinum-haired, tan-skinned woman clad in a trim, yellow uniform. I had seen her numerous times. But her name had, for the moment, lost itself somewhere in the twirls of fog.

"Good morning, Cammy." She went brusquely to open the drapes and I closed my eyes against the blast of light that shot into the room, disturbing its watery grayness.

"Chicken!" The woman gave a disapproving little laugh. "You are going to have to face the light sometime. Actually, it's gorgeous outside in the patio."

"Courtyard," I said defensively. Surprisingly the word made sense.

"Yes. I suppose you could call it that." I detected an alertness in the woman's voice, a note of expectancy. "Tell me about that other courtyard, Cammy. The one you remember."

Her words came as a shock and I opened my eyes to stare out through the gleaming doors. I had a brief impression of laving, green shadows and people moving through their coolness.

"Vines," I said. "There should be vines."

"What sort of vines, Cammy?" The woman's voice was cautious, the voice of someone watching a timid bird that might fly off at the least disturbance.

The thought distracted me and I lay quietly, wondering how I had imagined vines when there was only a sterile newness beyond the doors, a

13

newness that not even the espaliered trees could disguise.

"Ivy perhaps?" the woman prompted.

Vaguely I visualized impersonal, three-fingered leaves. There was no reason why there should be ivy. I mentioned this casually, knowing that the blond woman would be disappointed.

"What sort of vines *would* you prefer, then?"

"Grape." My lips formed the word effortlessly. "Zinfandels to be precise." I closed my eyes, glimpsing dappled green shadows, smelling for the briefest instant a familiar pungence slightly tainted with sulfur.

"Grapevines, Cammy?" A note of excitement had come into the woman's voice.

"Zinfandels." The word seemed odd this time. I wondered if it had meant anything, after all.

Someone had told me that it would happen like this, bits and pieces of memory pushing through the gray haze when I least expected them, often as not entirely out of context and not quite making sense. It had been a man's voice. Nate's, perhaps, or Dr. Simmons'. Doctor. The word distracted me.

"Sick people need doctors," I said. Then asked abruptly, "Who are you?"

The woman gave me a patient look. "You know very well who I am."

"Lesley." The name popped into my mind unexpectedly.

Lesley flashed me a triumphant smile. "You're doing better," she said. "Much better."

"You're a nurse," I said. "Sick people need doctors and nurses." A latent feeling of fear pushed through the gray lassitude and I forced myself to sit upright in the bed.

A girl with large, green eyes and a mass of long, tawny hair stared at me from across the room. I gasped, my hand flying to cover my mouth. The girl's hand flew up in unison with my own and I realized that it was myself sitting there in all of that wild dishevelment of hair, staring back from the shimmering depths of a floor-length mirror. I might have been blinking into a stranger's startled eyes.

The fog threatened to envelop me and I made a tremendous effort to hold it at bay. It seemed suddenly imperative that I find out where I was. Why? I surveyed the room frantically, really seeing it for the first time. A blast of color bombarded my senses. Yellows. Oranges. Reds. Beyond the French door people came into view, a man wearing a burgundy dressing gown and a woman with long, graying hair. They seemed vaguely familiar and I knew that they had been there before, drifting across my line of vision with no more impact than leaves carried on the wind.

Now I noticed that they seemed odd. The man squatted beside the path, carefully piling the white pebbles into neat little stacks, while the woman moved restlessly around the umbrella table shifting the striped chairs in an endless succession.

I cringed back against my pillows, overcome by a sudden sense of horror. "What is this place?" I demanded of Lesley.

"A hospital." Her voice was calm. "Jonas E. Gladstone Memorial. Does that ring any sort of bell?"

"Nurses in hospitals wear white," I said.

"This is a different sort of hospital." She smoothed her crisp, yellow garb over firm hips in a little gesture of pride. "A private institution, very swank and modern."

Opulent, I thought, managing to say the word properly aloud as I watched Lesley draw the drapes against a block of sunlight that crept insidiously over a gold-toned rug. The drapes, I noticed, were of some slippery, watered material that shimmered in all of the coruscating glory of a sunburst. The brightness hurt my eyes and I turned my head, wondering how I could possibly have imagined that the room was gray.

A nagging worry began to pry at me as I let my gaze rove around the room, taking in the richness of golden wood, the blended perfection of paintings that were unmistakably originals depicting full-blown salmon and yellow roses, their petals thick, loose splashes of paint clinging precariously to the canvas.

16

I managed at last to pin the worry down and said, "I can't afford any of this."

"How do you know that?" Lesley demanded.

"It's . . ." I fumbled for a word. Then gave up with a helpless nod. "I don't know. It doesn't make sense, does it, when you consider how little else I can grasp."

"Concentrate," Lesley commanded me. "Don't you want to know who you are? Who your family is? I'm curious, if you're not."

"It hurts," I murmured, knowing even as I uttered the words that it was an excuse. Beneath the pain and confusion lay a nameless threat, curled like a serpent waiting to strike. I hadn't the least idea how I knew that, either. But I knew.

Deliberately I closed my eyes against Lesley's insistent, yellow presence, willing the fog to wash over me. It came and I yielded myself to it gratefully, letting it carry me away from Lesley's voice that was calling my name over and over again.

Chapter Two

When I opened my eyes Nate Bantry had returned and was holding my hand.

"Cammy." He smiled warmly at me.

I stared up blankly at him, wondering how long he had been hovering over me, watching.

"That's you. Remember? Cammy Corwin," he said.

Cammy Corwin. I closed my eyes, trying desperately to associate the name with the lion-maned girl I had seen in the mirror. I refused to open them again until he had gone.

Then I asked Lesley who he was.

"It's working," she said obscurely. "Nate Bantry's fatal charm." She gave a knowing little laugh.

The room's exuberant colors swam around me in waves. Even with my eyes closed I could *feel* the vivid oranges and reds and yellows as though some dormant sense had been reawakened by Nate Bantry's persistent presence. *Sunshine dissipating fog, burning it into nebulous tendrils of steam writhing away between the vines, leaving the red dust damp and as dark as blood.* . . . The memory was no more than a teasing echo.

"Don't you remember him at all?" Lesley was asking.

"Remember who?" I had lost the thread of our conversation.

"Nate Bantry. Who else? After all, he is your employer. He had hired you, I understand, only a day or two before the accident. You were to have been his secretary. He expects you to assume your

18

duties just as soon as you feel up to it. Dr. Simmons has assured him that it won't be long."

"Nate Bantry," I said, testing the name. It meant no more now than it had in the beginning. "Is he the only one who has . . . ?" My voice trailed off, as it so often did, into vagueness.

"Come forward to identify you?" Lesley nodded. "You don't know how lucky you are to have an employer who takes an active interest. Especially under the circumstances. By the way, Dr. Simmons says you may leave your bed at any time. It's up to you. We'll get you into a wheelchair whenever you feel up to it."

"Wheelchair?"

"It's the only way with that broken ankle. The cast weighs a ton. And you're weak from lying in bed all these weeks. You were in a coma for over a month after the accident."

She had mentioned the accident before and the word hadn't penetrated. This time it did and I became conscious of the dead weight on my leg that seemed like an anchor pulling me out of the gray fog to pin me to earth. Exactly what *had* happened? The nameless threat hovered over me like a dark cloud, coupled with an agonizing expectation of sorrow and pain, and I found that I didn't want to think about it. I said instead, "Surely there was someone. Friends. Famy." I knew the word wasn't right and tried again, "Famby."

"Family," Lesley said with precision. "I've told

19

you. Nate Bantry is the only one. He brought you to us, as a matter of fact."

I had a sudden memory of the man I had seen piling pebbles beyond the French doors and the wild-haired woman who seemed compelled to shift the striped chairs endlessly around the umbrella table. I said, "This place . . . it's a mental institution, isn't it? Am I that bad?" I added tremulously.

Lesley looked blank for an instant. Then the patient smile illuminated her face and she said, "Not at all. You are improving rapidly. It's only a matter of time."

"Com . . . Commeted. That's the word, isn't it, when someone . . ." I broke off with a shudder.

"This isn't one of those horrid, snake-pit places, if that's what you are thinking. And the word is committed. You nearly had it. Jonas E. Gladstone Memorial is a private sanitarium. We provide specialized care for all sorts of cases. Everything from broken bones to manic depressives. Most of you will leave here eventually, capable, ready to become a part of things again."

Lesley's use of the nominative struck me. "It's not just my ankle," I said. "Someone told me about the other. The am . . . amnesty. It must have been Dr. Simmons."

"Amnesia. Anterograde amnesia," Lesley corrected me. "But don't let the big words frighten you. It means loss of memory following severe shock or trauma. In almost every instance it's only a temporary lapse."

"And I am here to wait it out," I said.

"That depends on Mr. Bantry. He's the one who is paying for all of this. Jonas E. Gladstone doesn't come cheap. One reason he's anxious to get you out of here."

"He mentioned taking me away?"

Lesley nodded. "In which case I suggest you try getting into the wheelchair soon. Today. We'll wheel you out into the patio with the others. What do you say?" She bustled around the room, opening a closet, taking out garments I had never seen. Or couldn't *remember* having seen. . . .

The dress she laid out was green with a row of crystal buttons glistening on its bodice. There were shoes in the same apple-green shade with blocky heels in what Lesley referred to as the latest fashion.

"Your Mr. Bantry was good enough to bring you a few things," she said, when I inquired about the clothes. "He has very definitely taken you under his wing."

I had a sudden, dark doubt. What part had Nathan Bantry played in my former life that warranted all of this—the costly room complemented by Lesley's chic, yellow-clad presence and the clothes racked in the spacious closet? I had glimpsed a raft of them lined neatly on the gleaming rod when Lesley opened the door. It seemed a good deal to expect from one's employer.

"I wish I could remember," I said.

"That's encouraging," Lesley commented, slipping the green dress over my head.

The dress smelled new as though it had never been worn.

As I sat on the bed waiting for Lesley to bring the wheelchair, the telephone attached to the yellow wall panel emitted a clever little chime. The sound repeated itself insistently and I reached hesitantly for the receiver.

"Cameo?" A man's voice came to me, scarcely more than a hoarse whisper vibrating over the line.

A cold, trembling sensation swept through me. I recognized it as terror. There had been another voice like that once. I tried to remember when. Where?

"Cameo," the voice said again.

"My name is Cammy," I said after a long pause. "You have the wrong person."

"I don't think so. But I am willing to call you Cammy if it will make you feel better."

I wanted to hang up. But the possibility that the man might be someone from my past nudged its way into my mind, tempering the strange fear that gripped me. I said, "It's not important what you call me since I don't know you."

"Have you remembered anything?" the voice demanded.

"I . . . I don't know." The terror asserted itself, washing over me in waves.

"You've no memory. Right? Let's keep it that way. Don't try digging up a past for yourself. Let well enough alone if you know what's good for you. Otherwise . . . Cameo?"

"Who are you?" My head had started to throb and I thought for an instant that the fog would claim me.

Then the feeling passed and I heard the voice saying, "Let's just say that I'm a friend who has taken it upon himself to warn you. You'll be sorry if you let yourself remember." There was a sharp click at the other end of the line.

Lesley came in pushing a wheelchair with large, shiny wheels. They seemed to grin evilly at me and I shrank from them with a little cry, the receiver tumbling from my fingers onto the bed.

"What is it?" Lesley's voice was edged with impatience as she hung up the phone. "Was it the police asking questions?"

I managed to shake my head. "A man. He threatened me. I can't go out there. I'm afraid."

"You have to leave this room sometime." Lesley seemed maddeningly unconcerned as she pushed the wheelchair into place beside the bed.

"You think that I . . ."

"That you are imagining things. Avoiding the issue, if you will. I know it's not easy to rejoin the world with no background. But it has to be done.

23

Keep in mind that sooner or later something will happen to jar your memory."

"I've changed my mind," I said. "I don't want to remember." Then, pleadingly, "Isn't there someone you can ask about the call. A switchboard operator?"

"Dr. Gladstone would never permit monitoring. Now. You are going outside." Lesley's manner made it quite clear that she didn't believe me and I was overcome by a sagging sense of weariness.

The frightening thing was that it was just possible I had imagined the whole thing, including the inexplicable waves of terror that had washed over me. It was hard to know what was real and what wasn't. Somewhere along the way the dividing line had become hopelessly blurred.

The woman who had been shifting the striped chairs stopped to stare as Lesley pushed the wheelchair swiftly over the pebbled path.

"Cinderella," she said, her gaze darting to the single green shoe I wore.

The man squatting beside the path counting pebbles glanced up and Lesley introduced us as though we were all in complete control of our mental faculties. The man was Mr. Kindel, Lesley said. Immediately the woman, whose name was Nora Jeeter, protested.

"Midas," she insisted in a shrill voice. "King

Midas counting his gold." She pointed toward the neatly stacked pebbles.

Lesley left me alone with them then and a sense of panic gripped me when I realized that I hadn't the least notion how to maneuver the chair. I tried the wheels and managed after a short struggle to roll myself away from them. Nora Jeeter trailed after me.

"What's the matter, honey?" She placed herself straddle-legged in the path of my wheelchair. "Do we scare you, Midas and me? The nurse should have told you. We're all harmless here. They don't accept the dangerous ones. Only the rich and innocuous. I'm loaded, you know. You run out of things to do when you're loaded. Like Midas. Nothing to do but count his gold."

"You're mad," I said.

Nora agreed with a happy nod. "And you. You've got no memory. Like Sleeping Beauty waiting for her prince. I've seen him in there with you, sitting beside your bed, kissing you. Except you didn't wake up. Maybe he doesn't know you're Cinderella and that he has to try the other slipper."

"Kissing?" I blinked up stupidly at her.

"Twice. Maybe more when the curtains were pulled." Nora gave a sly laugh.

An overwhelming question entered my mind: Had Nate Bantry been more to me than an employer back in that other time that had somehow eluded me? Was that why the sound of his voice

25

possessed a power to lift me out of gray lethargy? Love. I considered the word briefly, then brushed it aside telling myself that Nora was no doubt lying. Perhaps not intentionally, but lying nevertheless.

"How did you know about my memory?" I asked.

"It was in the paper. You're not really Sleeping Beauty at all. Or Cinderella either. You're some new character they've invented. The Cameo Girl."

"My name is Cammy," I said childishly.

Had it been Nora Jeeter on the telephone, I wondered, making mischief because she had nothing better to do? I wanted to believe that was all there was to it. But the impression remained that it had been a man's voice.

"It's as good a name as any, I suppose." Nora had lost interest. I watched her go back to her chairs and begin moving them around the table.

When Lesley appeared to wheel me back inside I asked her rather desperately when Nate Bantry was coming again.

She laughed. "He'll be back, never fear. You've become quite an investment at the prices they charge here. You must be a marvelous secretary." She paused, flashing me that same knowing look. "Say, you are really perking up, aren't you? Have you by any chance recalled the part your Mr. Bantry of Bantry Brut fame played in your former life?"

"Bantry Brut?"

"One of California's more popular wines," she explained. "Ruby red, but not quite a claret according to our expert, Dr. Simmons. Too tart and fruity, he says. I find it delightful nevertheless. Very relaxing. Your Mr. Bantry is more than generous, as I've said before. He presented the current Dr. Gladstone with an entire case of his rarest vintage. To be shared by staff, of course. A small token of his appreciation for the fine care we have given you. I asked Dr. Simmons a question or two, by the way. It happens that Bantry Brut is the end product of Zinfandels. Your remembering the name of that particular grape seems to tie everything up nicely."

I remained silent, attempting to digest what Lesley had said, as she wheeled me through the French doors into my room. The door leading into the hallway inched open. "She decent?" a man's voice asked.

Before Lesley could reply, Dr. Simmons stepped into the room and slid with a weary sigh into an orange chair that stood beneath one of the splashy paintings. He was a small, wiry man, his face seamed below a receding hairline, his eyes a piercing blue between wrinkled lids.

"Good to see you stirring," he remarked when Lesley had left the two of us alone. "That dress is very becoming. Green is a good color for you. Do you wear it often?"

"Is it the color I was wearing when . . ." I broke

27

off, dismayed by the sudden thought that I hadn't the least idea what my tastes had been.

"You had on yellow." Dr. Simmons took out a pack of cigarettes and held them casually toward me.

I shook my head. "Is that why I was put in this room? Everything is so vivid. You thought I liked bright colors."

"Not necessarily, although they might have helped you in time."

"Might have?"

"Mr. Bantry is growing impatient. He wants to take you away soon." Dr. Simmons seemed displeased by the idea.

"Must I go with him?" I asked, remembering what Nora Jeeter had told me.

"The man has assumed full financial responsibility for you."

"In other words I am indebted to him."

"Something like that. We're not a charitable institution."

"And if I should choose not to go with him," I began a little desperately.

"For some unimaginable reason the state has appointed him your guardian until such a time as you are able to function more or less normally. Or until your memory returns and you realize exactly who you are and what your place is in the scheme of things. According to the information Mr. Bantry has given us you are above the age of consent."

I had a sudden thought. "If he knows who I am, Mr. Bantry must know my family!"

"We'd have contacted them long before this if that were the case," Dr. Simmons said. "Sorry, Cammy. But Mr. Bantry seemed vague when it came to details. He claims you lived alone in San Francisco at a rather tacky address. The police went to check it only to find that the place had burned to the ground the night before you were found. The woman who leased to you was a cripple of some sort. She didn't get out in time and any clues that might have been in your apartment to confirm Mr. Bantry's identification have been lost. The police were up against a blank wall. They had only Mr. Bantry's word and the application form he claims you filled out for him to go on. Actually, anyone could have—" Dr. Simmons bit off his words suddenly, giving me a keen look. "Does any of it ring a bell?"

I shook my head disbelievingly.

"It seems ironic that the building housing your apartment should have burned just then. There'd been some sort of minor riot in the area and someone tossed a Molotov cocktail through a window. The police marked it off as part of the aftermath. But it could have been anyone." He leaned toward me a little, his face eager. "It's up to you to tell us your real name."

"Cammy," I said. "Cameo."

"No." He shook his head sadly. "We've only been calling you that because of the brooch."

"What brooch?"

He left me briefly and returned with two pins cupped in the palm of his hand, one of them a tiny, gold square with the numerals 120 raised on its face in black enamel. The other was a salmon-colored cameo, a woman's classic features carved on it in white. He gave them both to me.

"The brooch was pinned to your collar when you were found," he said. "The other is a short-hand award and was attached to your blouse. Apparently you are very adept."

"But I thought Mr. Bantry knew . . ." I broke off, turning the brooch over in my hand.

There were initials engraved on the back of the worn gold setting. S.H. and C.B. They were intertwined with a short message of undying love. They meant nothing to me.

"Mr. Bantry claims Cameo *is* your real name," Dr. Simmons was saying. "Odd that it should be the same as the name the newspaper people gave you. The Cameo Girl. It made a colorful story while it lasted." There was a note of sarcasm in his voice.

"I want to see it," I said.

"There was only one brief installment before Mr. Bantry stepped in to spoil their fun. His claiming to have a connection with you took away the intrigue and mystery. They had to go back to writing about the hippies for drama."

"What about my surname? Corwin?"

"Mr. Bantry provided that as well," Dr. Simmons said.

"The accident?" I forced myself to ask. "Tell me what happened."

"You don't remember any of it?"

"No."

"You were found by skin divers who were collecting abalone off the rocks below Fort Ross. You were caught on a cliff. Evidently you'd fallen."

Fort Ross. The name was only vaguely familiar.

"Where is this place?" I asked.

"A hundred miles or so up the coast. We've no idea how you came to be there along that isolated stretch of headland. There was no car. Nothing. Fortunately there happened to be a patch of shrubbery growing out of a projection along the face of the cliffs where you apparently went over. You landed in it pretty well battered. Popular theory has it that you were driving a car, lost control on one of those hairpin turns, and were somehow flung free as the car plunged into the sea. The tides along there are too fierce for any sort of dragging operation. So it must remain only a surmise. But a plausible one."

"It all sounds incredible," I said.

"Yes. Yes it does, for all of Nate Bantry's gallant efforts to give you an identity."

"You don't like him, do you?"

"That is beside the point. Professionally speaking, a restful country setting should do wonders for you and it is not as though you are *non compos mentis.*"

"But if I'm to work as his secretary . . ." I began.

"Apparently he maintains an office at his grape farm, which is located on some isolated mountainside near Napa. You'll live and work there at Vinecroft. The job must have held some appeal for you or you'd not have applied."

Vinecroft. I sat concentrating on the name after Dr. Simmons had gone. Like so many others, it meant nothing.

I became aware of Nate Bantry's presence even before he stepped into my room.

"Today is to be the day then," he commented, smiling down at me in my wheelchair.

I stared blankly up at him. Could I believe what Nora Jeeter had told me, I wondered. Was it true that he had kissed me while I lay locked in a gray stupor? Took advantage of me, I thought dramatically. Dismayingly the thought pleased me.

"Well, aren't you going to say something?" Nate demanded.

"I'm sorry," I said. "I slip off sometimes. It's hard not knowing what is real and what is imagination."

"I am taking you out of this place now that you are up and around. *That* is for real, I assure you."

He smiled at me, looking as though he lived in the sun.

I thought again how brown he was. Tawny. The word came bubbling from behind the gray curtain, trailing a memory that floated through my mind as detached as the gauzy message of a skywriter. *Don't look on the wine while it's red. Wait until it has begun to acquire that certain, clear tawniness. . . .* Had Nate Bantry implanted that particular bit of lore in my mind while I lay wrapped in my cotton-wool world? Or was it something that I had already known?

It seemed somehow significant that what few snatches of memory had come to me should deal with grapes. Nevertheless, I said, "I don't have to come with you. Dr. Simmons says I am past the age of consent."

He laughed. "Do you know what it means?"

A heat wave swept over me. "Yes. Of course."

"One thing you haven't forgotten is how to blush," he said.

"But how can you be sure that I can remember how to type and keep books? And the other . . . the fast writing," I ended lamely. I had intended my words to be a retort of sorts. But my stumbling tongue spoiled any effect I might have hoped to achieve.

"Dr. Simmons assures me in his pedantic way that certain motor skills are retained by amnesia victims. I've great faith in your competence."

"And if everything suddenly comes back to me

while I am at Vinecroft and I decide that I'd rather be elsewhere, after all? There has to be someplace, you know. Someone." My tone of voice had become slightly desperate. "I've only to conshen . . . concentrate."

"Don't." Was there a harsh note in his voice, or did I only imagine that sharp, cutting edge?

I blurted accusingly, "Why don't you want me to remember?"

"No particular reason." He became involved with cigarettes and a lighter that wouldn't work and was no longer looking at me.

"You know something about me," I said. "Something you haven't told."

"How much have they told you here?" he asked casually.

"Nothing other than that I am Cameo Corwin and was found on the sea cliffs near Fort Ross. Is there more? What do you know? You've no right—" My voice was rising shrilly and I broke off, swallowing in an attempt to control it. "I need to know," I added more calmly.

"You're sure you want to?" His eyes burned into me.

"There *is* something, then."

He nodded. "It's unpleasant, I'm afraid. We suspect that you may have tried to kill yourself."

"We?"

"The police. The state social officials. Those of us involved in your welfare."

"Kill myself?" It had taken a moment for the

harsh words to penetrate and now that they had I was overcome by a strong feeling of revulsion. "But that's unthinkable!"

"Which could account for your refusing to remember. Amnesia can be a way to avoid unpleasantness. Do you understand now why I've been telling you not to force it? That sort of thing has to be fought on equal ground and you're not girded for that battle just yet. The amnesia proves it."

"Did I say anything to you before the . . . accident?"

He hesitated and I sensed that he was still holding something back. "When I applied for the job," I prompted. "I must have contacted you and we talked."

"There was nothing to indicate that you were disturbed." He shrugged, snubbing out his cigarette and reached for another in the same motion. "Amnesia," he said then. "Nature's safety valve, shutting things up tight. My advice is to go along with it."

Someone cleared his throat nearby and Dr. Simmons stepped into the room. "Very interesting theory, Mr. Bantry," he said and I realized that he had been listening outside in the hall. "Hardly original. But interesting. Not from my own school of thought, however. And Cammy happens to be my patient, not yours. You've no right to interfere."

"You are mistaken, Doctor," Nate said. "I have a hundred-dollar-a-day right, as a matter of fact. That, I feel, entitles me to voice an opinion. I intended that Cammy's physical wounds be treated when I brought her here, no more. I'm certain Dr. Gladstone understood that if you didn't."

The case of wine Lesley had mentioned, I thought. Bribery of some sort? What did this sun-baked man want of me?

Dr. Simmons' eyes blazed. "You have gone to a good deal of trouble and expense to acquire a secretary, Mr. Bantry. Frankly this causes me to wonder just what sort of clever little game you are playing. What wild tale did you spin for the authorities to persuade them that you had some right to govern this girl's life?"

"That, Dr. Simmons, is none of your concern," Nate said coldly.

The small man spun away from us and rushed off down the hall.

"Damn him," Nate muttered. He turned to me. "I've arranged for your release. We're going home."

"Home?" My mind fumbled for some magic formula that would bring order to my confusion.

He nodded. "Yes home, dammit. Vinecroft. Are you afraid?" His eyes barely contained some raging enthusiasm.

"Should I be?" I felt infantile, needing comfort

and reassurance at the moment more than food and clothes and a roof.

Nate regarded me quietly for a long instant and I fancied suddenly that I saw some dark doubt lurking behind his eyes. As though, I thought crazily, he were the one who was frightened.

Then he smiled and said, "Not really. After all, you have me to watch out for you." There was a curious, fatalistic note in his voice, seeming to imply that I was to be in his care for a long while.

I remembered then that I was indebted to him, and a quiver of apprehension went through me, coupled paradoxically with a tremulous sense of eagerness. How much of the world beyond the plush, sanitarium walls would be familiar to me I wondered. Would I know the wine farm where Nate grew his grapes? Zinfandels. The word was like a straw bobbing across the gray turbulence of my mind and I grasped it desperately, thinking that whether my remembering it proved to be significant or not, Nate was all I had.

We left that same afternoon for Vinecroft.

Chapter Three

It was only when the first of the vineyards came into view, mantling the rolling Napa Valley foothills, that I began to feel an inkling of familiarity with my surroundings. The vines had begun to take on autumn hues, rich patches of gold and bronze splashed over the dark greens like highlights in a painting. Broad-winged clusters of purple-black fruit hung heavily at their staked hearts.

"Zinfandels," I said.

Nate gave me a startled look. "The grape of mysterious parentage. It grows only in California. No one knows how it got here or where it came from."

"Like me," I said.

"Has it ever occurred to you that no one can ever really recapture his past. Who was it that said, 'Look not mournfully to the past. It comes not back again. Wisely improve the present. It is thine. Go forth.' Longfellow? Smart man whoever he was. The fact that you've misplaced the memory of your own past can be our secret. No one need know. It will be better that way. Do you understand me? The important thing is that you know where you are going." His face had become terribly intense, his voice commanding.

A shiver of apprehension went through me. I said, "Is it much farther?" thinking that he was mistaken. Vinecroft was only a meaningless name to me. I hadn't the least idea where I was going.

He pointed toward the gray-spined mountains that hemmed the valley on our right. "Vinecroft is up there," he said. "On one of those blue ridges."

Minutes later we left the main road, driving between towering ranks of eucalyptus that gave way to live oaks as the road twined seductively upward through small, secret valleys. We had gone perhaps a dozen miles when a tiny town appeared ahead, shelved precariously against the side of a dark mountain.

"St. Felicia," Nate said. "Our local port of trade. I've a stop to make. I promise not to be long."

Giant fig trees draped thick foliage over the uneven streets of the small town, cooling the sun's ardor. It was a picturesque place, I decided, its balconied buildings quite obviously relics from a bygone age.

"Quaint," I commented, pleased that the right word had come to me.

"As everything in these hidden valleys is," Nate remarked, stopping the car beneath one of

39

the giant trees. "Including Vinecroft. There are those who would like nothing better than to commandeer all of it, burn off the vineyards, and turn these slopes into acres of plate glass and concrete, another bedroom for San Francisco."

"But it's so isolated."

"Fifty minutes to the center of Market Street, a mere dash around the block to the confirmed commuter."

"It would be sacrilege," I stated impetuously.

"I hoped you'd feel that way," Nate said. His voice had become far more intense than the moment seemed to warrant, and I had the curious feeling of being drawn inescapably into an involvement with his own sentiments.

"And if I hadn't?" I asked, thinking that I must begin to assert myself more firmly if I were to overcome the hold he seemed to have gained over me during those hours he had spent beside my bed wooing me with his soft voice.

"The important thing is that you do. Cameo," he added softly, his gaze going to the brooch I wore pinned to the collar of the green dress. "May I see it?" he asked suddenly.

He reached to unfasten the clasp, his fingers hard against my throat. A queer tingling sensation burned beneath my skin.

"Here, let me," I said quickly.

I brushed his hand aside and unfastened the clasp, dropping the brooch obediently into his outstretched palm. He turned it over and read the initials aloud. "S. H. and C. B."

"I'm going to try and have it traced to find out who they are," I said.

"You'll be disappointed," Nate said. "This is obviously an antique. Whoever they were they must have lived a long while ago." He turned the brooch over in his palm, examining the clasp, adding casually, "You should have this repaired. The safety clasp is loose. And you wouldn't want to lose it. I'll see to it."

"If you think it is really necessary," I said.

"It is, take my word for it." He dropped the brooch into his breast pocket and got out of the car. "Anyway, cameoes are passé." He said through the window. "It would never do for you to wear it at Vinecroft."

With that he hurried off down the street, leaving me numb with bewilderment, certain that I had caught a dark note of warning in his voice. What had he meant to convey, I wondered, watching him enter a narrow, brick building that had the legend, St. Felicia County Bank, painted in Old English script on its tall facade. Why shouldn't I wear what I pleased at Vinecroft?

There seemed to be no answer to that and I focused my attention on the town's several small shops, their modern wares incongruous behind slim, fanlighted windows. A chipped sign with the words "James P. Lockridge, Attorney at Law" fading on it dangled above a concrete step hol-

41

lowed with long use. A short distance down the street stood the hotel, a prim, freshly painted building, its balcony hanging over its face like a beetled brow. Several pieces of luggage stood before it and a woman wearing beige emerged through the building's stained glass doors to stand hopefully beside them. She scanned the street with impatient eyes, her gaze alighting on Nate's car.

Suddenly she was running toward the black Mercedes, her high heels clamoring impatiently over the uneven walk. She paused briefly when she glimpsed me seated behind the windshield, a look of puzzlement blurring the look of anticipation that had been on her face. Then she came forward once more, her expression accusing, as though she couldn't imagine any possible reason for my presence in the gleaming car.

"Where is Jefferey?" she demanded almost before she had reached me.

"Jefferey?" I gave her a blank stare.

"Jefferey Collins, of course. This is his car, isn't it?" Her look dared me to deny it.

I said, "I was under the impression that it belonged to Nate Bantry."

"Nate? But of course! How dear of him to take time out from his monumental labors to come for me." A note of sarcasm echoed through her voice. "By the way, I don't believe we've met. I'm Sabrina. Sabrina Mason." Clearly, she expected the name to mean something to me.

"And I'm Cammy. Cammy Corwin." I watched her perfect features for a reaction.

She seemed as much at a loss as I was and I quieted any misgivings I might have had with the thought that Nate was hardly the type to discuss his business affairs indiscriminately.

"I suppose you've some perfectly logical reason for being here," Sabrina said, a slightly hostile speculation glowing in eyes that were startlingly dark against the soft beige tones of her hair.

"Yes. As a matter of fact I do."

"Don't tell me that Nate has acquired a romantic flair since I was last here," Sabrina commented. "Where is he, by the way. Claudia told me when I called the house that someone would definitely be on hand to greet me. I expected Jefferey or Sebastian. But Nate? Never!" She gave a brittle laugh. "What a bother it is to come by bus. There is no other practical way to reach this bestial place, however. Something will have to be done about that, of course, when the developers take over Vinecroft." I must have looked stunned, for she added, "Hasn't Nate told you? But no, I suppose he wouldn't."

"Told me what?" I asked.

"That we plan to sell the grape farm to a San Francisco firm for a rather fabulous price." She sounded confident, as though she had every right to share in the disposal of the vineyard that I had imagined, until now, belonged exclusively to Nate Bantry.

Would I be working for this expensively sharp woman as well, I wondered, thinking how gullible I had been in my eagerness for someone to cling to. It simply hadn't occurred to me to question Nate about his farm or his family. Perhaps because I had been afraid of what I might discover, not only about him but about myself as well.

Now I found myself wondering what part Sabrina Mason played in his life. I said, "You live at Vinecroft?"

"Periodically." Her tone of voice was noncommittal. "But to get back to Nate, darling. You haven't yet mentioned where he's gotten off to."

"He's at the bank," I said.

"I might have guessed. No doubt he's attempting to finagle another loan out of Old Man Greeves," Sabrina added irreverently. "In which case he may be a while. Our dear Mr. Greeves is notoriously tightfisted when it comes to money. Not that I blame him for being cautious when it comes to Nate." She gave me a deliberate look. "After all, Nate has nothing but the shirt on his back to put up for security. I sometimes wonder why I bother with him. Except that he is so damnably male. Don't you agree?" The sly smile curving her carefully lipsticked mouth was almost taunting.

"I was under the impression that Vinecroft belongs to him," I said numbly. "At least a part of it."

"You've been misinformed. The only thing

Nate can lay a legitimate claim to is Gain Bantry's name."

I thought disbelievingly of the expensive care Nate had provided for me, my mind groping blindly through its gray vacuum, trying to focus on some reasonable explanation. There was none and I stared out vacantly through the windshield, thinking how utterly foolish I had been to place my trust in a stranger simply because he had whispered comforting words to me. Who could I trust, I wondered. Was there someone somewhere . . .

"Darling, you look utterly demolished." Sabrina's voice broke in on my staggering thoughts. I fancied that I detected a small note of satisfaction in it. "I do believe you have been bamboozled. Under the circumstances it might be wise if we were to pool our information about my unpredictable cousin. It could be to our mutual advantage, don't you agree?"

"Nate is your cousin?" I said.

"Distant, darling. Very distant." Sabrina's smile revealed small, predatory teeth. "So don't go setting your hopes too high. That *is* why you are here, isn't it? To captivate Nate."

"I am Mr. Bantry's secretary," I stated, striving for dignity. My attempt failed miserably and I managed only to sound self-righteous and prim.

Sabrina flashed me a disbelieving look, then emitted a cutting laugh. "Come, now. You can't really expect me to believe that. The least we can do is to be honest with one another. You may as well confess your motives, darling. I've a wicked intuition when it comes to other women."

"Ask Nate," I retorted, feeling suddenly weary. If I willed it, would the protective bank of fog wash over me?

I closed my eyes and waited, hearing Sabrina say in a shocked voice, "You are absolutely serious, aren't you, darling? But Nate hasn't a nickel to his name. Whatever would he do with a secretary?" Then, sharply, "Darling, are you all right?"

The obliterating grayness failed to wrap itself around me and I opened my eyes. "Just tired," I said. Then in reply to Sabrina's question, "I'm to keep Mr. Bantry's records."

"Nate hasn't that many records to keep," Sabrina stated flatly. "He could keep tabs on the few gallons of wine he manages to produce on the sides of the vats. Tot them up in chalk." She pulled open the car door. "You may as well make room for me since I'll be going with you the rest of the way. In the meantime, I think it is time someone filled you in on the pertinent facts of life." She scooted in beside me, giving a little gasp when she saw my cast. "Nate always had a soft spot for birds with broken wings," she commented. "How did it happen?"

"An . . . accident," I said.

"You've courage, I must say. A girl in your condition allowing Nate to drag you off up here to the Bantry aerie. Has it occurred to you that you won't be able to run?"

"You mentioned someone named Gain. Gain Bantry," I said, ignoring the knowing look she gave me. "Is he Nate's father?"

"Nate's stepfather. My uncle." Sabrina smiled rather smugly. "So you see, Nate isn't actually my cousin at all, although we've always referred to each other in that vein."

"Then I suppose that I shall actually be working for Gain Bantry," I said hopefully.

"Hardly. Gain has been missing for nearly seven years."

"Missing?"

"He disappeared. Simply vanished into thin air. One of those weird cases you read about in the newspapers."

"But people don't just evaporate like water."

"But they do, darling. At least Gain seems to have done that. It was all terribly eerie, my uncle being the sort of man he was, riddled by superstition, always hiding out in his gloomy old wine cellars. They seem simply to have swallowed him."

"Surely there must have been some clue to his disappearance."

"Not unless you consider the fact that he emptied his safe a clue. Simply cleaned it out, taking whatever papers had been there with him. Vanished, papers and all, without a trace. In the meantime, Nate has attempted to preserve the

Bantry reputation for fine wines. It has become an absolute passion with him. These interminable loans he keeps begging off Old Man Greeves . . . he must owe thousands. Oh, here is my precious cousin now." Her gaze slid past me and I glanced out to see Nate hurrying toward the car, his eyes downcast, his face stormy.

I guessed that his visit to the bank had been unfruitful and tried not to think what my stay at Jonas E. Gladstone had cost him. A gloomy sensation went through me as Sabrina slid from the car and ran to throw possessive arms around his neck. I turned quickly away, focusing my gaze on a cluster of bare-legged children who played along the narrow street, darting like upright, brown lizards from one pool of shade to the next.

"Sabrina!" I heard Nate say, at last. He sounded surprised. But not joyous, I thought.

I was able then to look at them as they came toward me, Sabrina clinging to Nate's arm, demanding why he hadn't been at the hotel to greet her when her bus arrived.

"I hadn't the least idea you were coming," Nate said.

"But I thought—"

"Sorry to disappoint you," Nate interrupted her, "but I've been away. I couldn't have known."

"And Jefferey? This *is* his car, isn't it?"

Nate nodded.

"I thought so. Spit and polish are important to Jefferey. No doubt he's busy trying to wipe the

48

grime from your outdated Mercedes which explains why he's late. Claudia *did* promise that someone would come."

"My car is temporarily out of commission," Nate stated gruffly. "You'd have had to be content to ride in Sebastian's old truck if I hadn't happened along."

"God forbid!" Sabrina slid back in beside me. "How lovely it will be to have money again."

I guessed that she was referring to the sale of Vinecroft and a sense of desolation swept through me. I realized then how important it had been to me to have someplace definite to go, even though it had been only a meaningless name, and I wondered suddenly what was to become of me. It occurred to me that, by the mere act of continuing to sit dumbly beside Nate Bantry in the charging car, I was committing myself irrevocably to an unknown fate.

We left the town behind, the road continuing to twine upward through the vines, ranks and troops of them marching over the steep slopes. A winery of hewn stone loomed ahead, crowding beside the road, its sturdy walls mantled in ivy, the redwood shakes on its peaked roof weathered to a luminous shade. A cross stood at its apex, thrusting silvered wings against the azure sky. I wondered if I dared to consider it an omen and realized how dangerously shaken my faith in Nate had been by Sabrina's impromptu revelations.

Drawing a deep breath, I deliberately pushed

49

doubt from my mind, becoming suddenly aware of an achingly poignant sweetness. The concentrated, raisin tartness of ripe fruit blending into the dusty smells of tarweed and sulfur. ... I had known that peculiar aroma before, and my heart thudded as I felt myself hovering on the brink of some teasing chasm of memory.

"This damnable heat." Sabrina's voice drew me back abruptly. "I'd forgotten how hot it can be in these forsaken hills. Thank God for those storm clouds."

I glanced out and saw thunderheads building above the mountain tops.

"It can't rain now," Nate said. "We need this heat to preserve the bloom."

"Just like that," Sabrina commented. "Rain clouds go away because I don't need you just now." Her voice had become slightly mimicking. "You and those damned grapes. I should think you'd have tired by now of playing the gentleman farmer."

"You should realize by now that I am not playing games," Nate retorted.

Sabrina shot him a fiery glance. "Are you by any chance trying to intimidate me?" she said.

"I can hardly visualize anyone managing that," Nate commented.

Something seethed between the two of them that I couldn't quite grasp. I said nervously, "These vineyards we're passing now? Do they belong to Vinecroft?"

Nate nodded. "Over ninety thousand vines. I haven't been able to maintain them all as I'd have liked to. We'll have to buy new root stock next spring to replace those that have gone to wood." Dismayingly, his glance seemed to indicate that I was to share in that particular undertaking.

"You're wasting your breath," Sabrina said. "You know very well that Vinecroft is to be sold."

"Over my dead body," Nate said savagely.

We shot ahead in silence and after a while Sabrina said, "Jefferey was right, then. He came to see me last time he was in San Francisco. He told me then that you had become more fanatical than ever about the vines, that it was utterly hopeless to try to reason with you." Her voice softened a little. "It's not that the rest of us are unappreciative of what you've tried to do, darling, and I must admit that I enjoy a lovely claret now and then as much as the next one. But to slave as you do, Nate, when none of it actually belongs to you ... Racking your pitiful few gallons every fall, then foolishly putting your small proceeds, along with what few dollars you can manage to squeeze out of Old Man Greeves, into buying equipment that will be considered a part of the estate when everything is settled ... You won't have realized a thing for all your years of effort beyond a few horny calluses and a gross stack of I. O. U.'s." She shook her head disbelievingly. "Naturally Claudia won't let you starve. But you should look ahead. You should have started doing that the day

Gain ... went away. That is, if he is actually gone. Sometimes I wonder."

"What is that supposed to mean?" Nate demanded.

Sabrina gave a nervous little laugh. "I have the oddest feeling sometimes that he may be lurking in those moldy cellars, spying on all of us. I suppose it is because he was always rather strange. Or perhaps because you remind me of him at times."

Nate remained grimly silent. When I could no longer bear the sense of uneasiness that seemed to hover over us like a dark cloud, I said, "Surely some arrangement was made for the operation of the farm after the owner disappeared."

"Sabrina certainly wasted no time in filling you in on our family history," Nate commented. "What else did my erstwhile cousin tell you behind my back."

"That you are an absolute charlatan, for one thing," Sabrina said brightly. "Bringing this poor, crippled girl here on the pretense of needing a secretary when you've about as much use for one as Peter Pan."

I looked bravely at Nate. "I think I deserve to know your real reason for bringing me to Vinecroft," I said. I recalled that Dr. Simmons had disliked Nate Bantry; had seemed to suspect him of having some dark design on me. The thought had seemed preposterous at the time. Now I wasn't so certain.

Nate flashed me a fierce look. "I've not brought you all of this way to seduce you if that's what's in your mind. My motive goes much deeper than that."

"Motive?" I parroted, my face burning.

Sabrina gave a brittle laugh. "Really, darlings." I didn't miss the dark note of disapproval in her husky voice and was certain then that the undercurrent I sensed beneath their sullen contretemps was an attraction of sorts.

Beside me, Nate said, "I suggest that you take me at my word, Cammy. How else can we hope to establish a sensible relationship? I do intend to put you to work, I assure you, the instant you're up to it. It will be your job to keep tabs on every drop of must that passes through the lines."

"The language of the trade, darling," Sabrina commented dryly. "Nate may be a usurper. But he speaks with a vintner's tongue. A *soi-distant* authority on grapes, as the saying goes." There was a note of mockery in her voice.

"It remains to be seen which of us are usurpers at Vinecroft," Nate said.

"You surely haven't forgotten that your mother was . . . is Gain's wife," Sabrina remarked.

"No need to tiptoe around, Sabrina." Nate's face was grim. "I know Gain is dead."

Dead, a small voice echoed inside of me. *Dead*. It was an echo of my own voice, disbelieving, shot through with grief. Who had died? I wondered.

Who did that faint, inner voice mourn? Gain Bantry? But that was incredible. . . .

I forced myself to concentrate on what Sabrina was saying. "You sound terribly positive, Nate darling. As if you knew for certain that someone . . ." She broke off with a little shrug.

"Murdered him?" Nate said bluntly. "Face it, Sabrina. He wouldn't have walked out without saying something to *me*."

"Gain's golden boy," Sabrina commented. She looked at me, a maddening little smile playing over her full mouth. "Nate can't accept the fact that Gain was a bit odd. Walking out of the picture, once he had drawn up his will, was something my uncle would do. There *is* a will, you know, all properly signed and sealed. It will be opened and read the day Gain is declared legally dead by the courts. No one has the least inkling who will get what and it has made us rather edgy with each other, I'm afraid. In the meantime, Nate persists in this mad idea that Gain met with foul play, presumably at the hands of one of us there at Vinecroft. He has even managed to infect the town." She gave a convincing little shudder. "One reason I loathe spending any more time than necessary in that dull place. All those suspicious little eyes glaring at me. We are all suspect, you know. And that, darling, is merely one of our lively, family skeletons there at Vinecroft. The place is riddled with them. Is it any wonder that we shall all—with the exception of Nate, of course

—be glad to see the vines put to the torch and that hideous old house razed."

Nate looked straight ahead, without comment, a thunderous expression on his face. I sensed that his feeling for the grape farm was so intense that he didn't trust himself to speak.

Chapter Four

Vinecroft. The sign dangled between stone gateposts set into the shadows of monolithic live oaks. Beyond it, a drive wound through an aisle of greenery shot through with blinding shafts of sunlight. The car rounded a jutting spur of limestone and the trees opened to give a view of yet another vineyard spilling over the rolling slopes. An old house stood in its midst, protected from the sun by a phalanx of tall, shade trees.

There was a winery a little beyond and above the mansion, set into the hillside so that it seemed to grow there. Below the vineyards, the small, brown roofs of pickers' cabins poked above the greens and golds of the vines. The view over the valley far below was breathtaking, and I could well imagine a developer's eagerness to acquire

Vinecroft's slanting acres as the ideal site for luxurious homes away from megalopolitan madness.

The drive circled and Nate brought the car to a halt before a high veranda densely shaded by a great, twining vine. Something stirred in me and a fragment of memory burst free from the grayness that smothered my memory to float aimlessly through my mind. I squeezed my eyelids tight together in an effort to bring it more clearly into focus and glimpsed for a quavering instant the nebulous image of someone waiting patiently in green shadows. Someone whose presence filled me with a sensation of being wanted and loved.

I had the eerie feeling that I need only to open my eyes and my past would unfold from beyond the rough, green fronds that mantled Vinecroft's old-fashioned veranda. Then suddenly I was seized by an inexplicable feeling of dread. I must have uttered some small, panicky sound, for Nate said in an anxious voice, "Cammy! Are you all right?"

I sucked in a steadying breath. I said, "It was only a twinge in my ankle," the thought burning in me that Nate had warned me against remembering. I wasn't certain that I wanted to bring back my past as I sat staring fearfully into the green shadows beneath the vine.

Sabrina had alighted from the car to run lightly up the broad steps, and a man emerged to greet her. I seemed to recognize him, and my heart lurched.

56

When he had released Sabrina, he stood smiling down at Nate and me, a wary expectancy gleaming in his eyes. I read cynicism in his crooked smile and something else that escaped me. I held my breath half-expecting him to call me by name.

"My brother, Jefferey." Nate gave him an identity.

I realized then that, although the man was older than Nate and of a different complexion—sandy-haired in contrast to Nate's bold darkness—their features were very similar. It had been this resemblance that I had recognized. Inexplicably, this realization filled me with a feeling of relief.

"Jefferey Collins," the man said, running down the steps. "Unlike my brother, I preferred to retain our father's name. And you, my dear? Who might you be?" He watched me closely with eyes that were a brooding shade of green.

"Brace yourself, Jefferey," Sabrina said, "Nate has hired himself a secretary. Cammy. Cammy Corwin."

"Secretary!" A voice echoed out of the shadows beyond Sabrina, and a tiny, blond woman appeared. She glared down at Nate who had gone around the car to lift out my wheelchair. "Have you lost your mind?"

"That, dear Mother, is a moot question," said Jefferey dryly. "Nate has always behaved like a damned fool." He turned his attention back to me. "Cammy. Short for Camille, I suppose."

I started to speak, then caught Nate's quick, cautioning glance and fell silent, something he had said to me earlier running crazily through my mind: *Cameos are passé.* Why hadn't he wanted me to wear the brooch, I wondered. The quick look he had given me had told me as clearly as though he had spoken his thoughts aloud that I wasn't to reveal my name. A sense of intrigue went through me and I sat marveling that he could, with a glance, convey his wishes to me so completely. Had he acquired some weird power over me, I wondered. The idea amazed me in that I found it rather pleasing. At the same time, an insidious fear crept through me.

Nate was introducing me to his mother. "Claudia," he called her. "Claudia Bantry."

I gave a little nod, seeing bitterness imprinted clearly on her heart-shaped face.

"This is impossible," she said. "I can't imagine why Nate has placed us all in this awkward position." She turned on him. "You can't be serious." Her eyes that were the same color as Jefferey's searched his face almost frantically. As though, I thought, she doubted his sanity.

Nate seemed oblivious to her harsh scrutiny, turning to scan the uneven horizon on the far side of the valley. The billowing clouds had lost some of their soft purity, taking on an angry, gray tinge around their edges. Although the sun continued to shine in their midst, a hint of moistness had come into the air. I fancied that I smelled rain.

"Damn," Nate muttered. "I don't like the looks of that weather. The Rieslings can't take it." He paused for an instant, his brown hands braced on his hips, then struck off decisively up the slope in the direction of the winery.

I stared helplessly after him.

"I suppose it is up to us to do something about getting Cammy inside," Sabrina said. "She's crippled." Her tone of voice seemed to indicate that I could very well prove to be a nuisance.

It was suddenly unthinkable that I should remain here to be patronized, even insulted by these people who seemed to harbor a dark, underlying suspicion of each other. And of me, I couldn't help thinking, wondering if one of them actually had murdered the missing Gain Bantry.

The thought sent a shiver through me. I said, forcing firmness into my voice, "I shan't stay where I'm not needed."

I would manage somehow, I consoled myself. Dr. Simmons had, at the last minute, thrust a crisp bill into my hand—out of some distorted sense of conscience, I had suspected at the time. It was tucked now into the new purse Nate had provided, affording a short-ranged security of sorts. Nate could hardly stop me from going, I thought. I was, after all, above the age of consent, according to him, and in my right mind now that

59

I had come out of the fog. I would find a room somewhere, advertise for typing jobs. Even as my mind hastily devised the plan, I realized how impractical it was.

It was with a feeling of release that I heard Jefferey saying gallantly, "But of course you're staying! My God, we must seem an inhospitable lot. It's just that we're rather unsettled right now. *None* of us will be at Vinecroft much longer. In the meantime, it will be inspiring to have a new face gracing the premises."

Claudia looked helplessly at Jefferey, making no effort to conceal her displeasure, as he opened the car door, revealing my ankle in its unsightly cast. I allowed him to help me out, thinking: *Time. All I need is a little time.* I wondered why I hadn't realized before what a precious commodity it was. All of those days spent drifting aimlessly in fog when I should have been concentrating as Lesley and Dr. Simmons had asked, taking stock of myself.

"It was unforgivable of Nate to stalk off like that," Sabrina said. "It's those damned grapes. He's definitely obsessed."

"We'll manage without him." Jefferey leaned over me with a conspiring smile. "You must have had quite a spill to do this to yourself," he added, adjusting my cast on the footrest of the wheelchair.

"Yes. Yes I did," I said, gratitude blotting out

any reasonable opinion I might have formed of Nate's older brother.

I suppose that I was, in a way, attracted to him. For one thing, his voice was remarkably like Nate's. And it had been Nate's voice that had first drawn me to *him,* luring me out of the empty, gray caverns where I had taken refuge. It had seemed, then, to hold some worthwhile promise.

Now, I wondered suddenly if I had only imagined tenderness in him as Jefferey wheeled me to the foot of the veranda steps. Without warning, Jefferey lifted me, chair and all, and bore me upward. Although I realized that I must have lost a good deal of weight during the past weeks of grayness, his strength seemed slightly monumental.

Behind us, Sabrina clapped her hands and cried, "Bravo!"

"You'd no idea how strong I am, had you, Cousin," Jefferey commented slyly.

Only Claudia remained grimly silent, going to open the mansion's stained-glass door. The glittering mosaic of leaded color had been set, unbelievably, to form a full-length portrait of a gallant from some past age. An errant beam of sunlight found its way through the meshed leaves of the big vine to illuminate the life-size figure as we passed into the house, so that the eyes seemed to glare down at me with some fiendish malice.

I had the sudden feeling that I was caught up in an incredible nightmare from which there was no escape, as Jefferey wheeled me into an immense foyer that was as darkly foreboding as a crypt.

Chapter Five

For all of its Victorian gloominess, the old house must once have been elegant. Dark, gleaming woods formed a high, carved wainscoting around the large foyer that had doors opening off it on all sides. At its far end, a stairwell curved upward to a landing that was illuminated by a round, stained-glass window set with a picture of three handsome stags painted on frosted glass. A feeble fire flickered in a tiled fireplace at one side, casting its faint glow across a parquet floor.

A door opened silently beneath the curve of the stair and a girl appeared, her face blending into the brown shadows. I realized that she was Mexican.

"Maria!" Jefferey's voice sounded startled. "What are you doing here?"

"Nate sent me." The girl's voice was soft. Unaccented.

"Mr. Bantry, if you please," snapped Claudia.

"How many times must I remind you? The fact that my son insists on making himself common is no excuse for you to forget your place in this household."

The girl stood quietly, her stony endurance exuding defiance in its most indefatigable form.

"Mr. Bantry asked me to see to Miss Corwin," the girl said, when Claudia had grown silent. "She's to be put in the library, since there are no sleeping rooms on the ground floor." Only her eyes seemed to hold some brooding resentment.

It might have been directed toward any one of us, I thought, myself included. Although it hardly mattered to me then whether the girl liked me or not. The important thing was that Nate hadn't forgotten me. His Rieslings hadn't come first, after all. My heart soared on a surge of triumph.

"I'm still mistress of this house," Claudia was saying in her imperious voice.

"Well, Mother?" Jefferey asked expectantly. I glanced up to see the crooked smile playing around his mouth in what appeared to be mocking amusement. As though, I caught myself thinking, he were daring Claudia to counteract Nate's orders. "Where is it to be, then?"

"It will have to be the library, I suppose," Claudia conceded. "Until other arrangements can be made," she added, in a tone of voice that clearly indicated she expected my stay at Vinecroft to be short-lived.

Jefferey wheeled me along a dark corridor past

63

several closed doors carved, appropriately, in a pattern of trailing vines. Maria slipped ahead of us, pushing one of the doors open at last, and I was thrust into a large, dank room, its walls totally smothered by books.

"I'll send Sebastian with your luggage," Jefferey said. "In the meantime, I'm certain Maria will somehow manage to make you comfortable. She has quite a knack for that sort of thing." He chuckled wickedly.

The dark-skinned girl ignored his veiled insinuation, and I watched him disappear, an uncomfortable feeling sweeping through me that my existence was becoming more precarious by the moment. I had an inordinate desire to escape from Vinecroft and it was only my broken ankle that held me back. That, plus the fact that I had nowhere to go. Nor had I the least idea from what helf-sensed danger I might be running.

I slumped in my wheelchair, the surge of triumph I had felt at Maria's appearance obliterated by the oppressing room.

My despondency deepened when Nate failed to appear for dinner that night. I had caught a glimpse of him earlier through the library windows, hurrying into the vineyards, his muscular body clad unfamiliarly in tight-fitting jeans and a faded work shirt. A small, brown man had limped along beside him, the Sebastian Jefferey had mentioned, no doubt.

Now, as Maria wheeled my chair into place at the long table, Jefferey informed me that Nate would remain in the vineyards for as long as the light held, reaping the thin-skinned Rieslings that were so fragile they must be rushed almost instantaneously to the crusher.

"Lest they suddenly realize that they have been severed from their life-source and some hair-line balance in their chemistry is disturbed," Jefferey added mockingly.

He was at the head of the table in the place that I had first imagined must belong to his younger, more resourceful brother. And he was, I knew, quoting Nate about the perishable Rieslings. I would be fortunate, he went on to say, if I saw Nate even once a week throughout the remainder of the vintage. Most particularly if the rain clouds continued to threaten.

A childish feeling of abandonment came over me. I must have looked crestfallen, for Jefferey whispered cunningly, "You still have me, Cammy darling."

My face burned, and I glanced quickly at Claudia and Sabrina to see if they had heard. Sabrina was watching me, a wicked little smile curving her sensuous mouth.

"You have entered the wolves' lair," she said. "All that is lacking is your red hood." There was a biting edge to her voice.

I turned my attention to the plate Claudia passed to me, recalling that it had been Jefferey who had appeared at the library door with my luggage in lieu of the Sebastian he had mentioned. He had lingered for some time and I had been aware then that he was taking more than a casual interest in me. There had been something in his eyes that I didn't quite trust.

Now he said easily, "Pay no mind to Sabrina, Cammy. She is part witch as you shall soon discover for yourself."

"And you, darling, are the fallen angel himself," said Sabrina, with acid sweetness.

There was a pause as a rotund Mexican woman appeared to serve our meal.

"Carmelita, a bottle of our finest wine," Jefferey said airily. "Pinot Chardonnay should do nicely."

Nate's wine, I caught myself thinking defensively, as the woman hurried out.

"In case you are curious, Carmelita is Maria's mother," Sabrina said to me. "Sebastian's wife, and a jewel. Not at all like her daughter whom, you will soon discover, is recalcitrant and given to fits of moodiness. The family supposedly owned property here at one time, a Spanish land grant which they lost when California became a state. Their last name is, unbelievably, Revis-Gerara, one of the more noble Spanish names, according to Sebastian. He spins some grand tales about his ancestors. I've an idea they've turned Maria's head."

"The name does have a certain ring to it," I commented.

"Don't let Maria hear you admit it, or she may refuse to wait on you," Sabrina said.

"You are attaching far too much importance to Maria's presence in this household," Claudia said. "After all, she is only a servant regardless of what her family might once have been."

"I can't imagine why you tolerate her, Claudia," Sabrina said.

"Out of deference to Nate, of course." said Jefferey, with a disapproving note in his voice. "Little by little, Mother has yielded her authority to him, whether she cares to admit it or not."

"It would be difficult to manage without Carmelita," Claudia said. "You know as well as I do that she wouldn't stay if I were to turn Maria out."

"And there is the matter of *Nate* needing Sebastian's services as a dresser of the vines, not to mention Maria's clever ministrations."

"That will do, Jefferey!" Claudia said sharply.

"Sorry, Mother." Jefferey's face broke into a winning smile.

Claudia's small face softened at once. There was no mistaking Jefferey as her favorite son, and I caught myself wondering in what incalculable way Nate had displeased her that she should seem so bitterly inclined toward her own flesh and blood.

For all of my misgivings, I found myself

67

growing increasingly curious about this strange household. Although none of them had seemed to recognize me upon my arrival at Vinecroft, an uneasy feeling persisted that my forgotten past was somehow tied up with their own, and I determined to learn all I could about Nate's family. That I had once lived on a grape farm, I was certain. The fact that I had remembered Zinfandels seemed to confirm this irrevocably. Furthermore, I was convinced that there had once been someone in my life who, like Nate, lived for the vines. Or was it *Nate Bantry* whom I half-remembered out of that other time before the accident. In which case, I told myself, there had been much more between us than he had cared to admit. Had I, for some incalculable reason, rebelled against him to the point of trying to destroy myself? Was that why he had warned me against trying to remember?

The questions churned uneasily through my mind, and I forced them aside with a little shudder, focusing my attention on Jefferey who was favoring me with one of his crooked smiles. Carmelita had arrived to place a slim, green bottle before him. He splashed the sparkling, white wine carelessly into tulip-shaped glasses and proposed a toast: "To the charming new addition to our household."

When we had all sipped obediently, he said, "I've an idea we'll get on famously once we've become better acquainted. Suppose you start the ball rolling, Cammy, by telling us a little something about yourself." Then, when I could only stare numbly at him, "Where did Nate find you, for instance? What about your family? The inessential details." He gave a careless flick with his well-manicured hand.

My senses reeled as I glimpsed more than a passing curiosity behind Jefferey's jade-colored eyes, and I fumbled for something to say.

"Darling, it's not as though Jefferey had asked whether or not you are sleeping with Nate," Sabrina prompted. "Or were before the cast," she added cattily.

"I'm from San Francisco," I said quickly, seeing a perverse curiosity flare in Jefferey's eyes. "I had an apartment there until I decided to come here to work for Mr. Bantry."

"Charming place. Definitely small town. But charming. I marvel that our paths haven't crossed. But then we wouldn't have moved in the same circles."

"Sabrina quite literally gyrates," Jefferey contributed. "Between here and there. And, of course, between husbands. She collects men as though they were trophies. Only the wary manage to escape her keen sights." He glanced at Sabrina. "I suppose your turning up here at this point means that you have shed the last one. Forgive me, darling. But I seem to have forgotten his name. Carl? Or was he number two?"

"Does it matter? The important thing is that I

69

am free of him. It turned out that he was a wastrel with barely a penny to his name." Sabrina made a dismissing gesture.

"And money is dreadfully important," Jefferey said, in that pseudo-mocking way of his.

"Utterly," Sabrina agreed. "I've a passion for rich men."

"And you, my dear?" Jefferey fixed me with a demanding gaze. "What sort of men do you prefer?"

I blinked at him, caught off my guard. What sort of man *had* I preferred? It was eerie not knowing, and a sense of unreality swept over me. Had I been attracted to someone like Nate, dark-haired and russet-skinned? Looking as though he had been steeped in cabernet. . . . The fanciful thought struck me. Cabernet. It was a wine, of course, another fragment of memory cropping out of the gray wall that obscured my mind.

I became aware of Jefferey's searching gaze and wondered in the next breath if it might have been someone like him who had appealed to me, his glossy charm enhanced by some dark current of intrigue.

"You should be considering men rather seriously at your age," Sabrina said. "By the way, how old are you, darling? I know it's impertinent to ask. But I am curious."

I hesitated, then said a bit too quickly, "Twenty. I'm twenty."

"I hope you've no illusions about Nate," said

Claudia unexpectedly. I had the feeling that her thoughts had been dwelling on her younger son throughout our conversation and that she was merely speaking them aloud. "He may have been born a Collins. But at heart, he is a Bantry." The name, spoken in her disillusioned voice, seemed to take on some dire meaning.

"I'm afraid I don't understand," I said.

"My God, darling. Surely you've heard of the Bantry legend," Sabrina said. I couldn't tell whether she was serious or was merely trying to startle me. "It's an integral part of California's stormy past, one of those classic scandals that is included in every gossipy history that has ever been written about our little corner of the world. It's become fashionable you know to trot out all of the old tales, the more shocking the better. Some new author—I forget his name—dug into the archives a few years back. He even went so far as to interview our own Sebastian who is overly fond of weaving wild tales. The result was a thing titled *Hidden Legends of the Mother-Lode,* or some such. Surely you've run into it."

"I don't really care for history," I murmured.

Jefferey gave me a curious glance. "I've a feeling Nate has been keeping secrets from you," he said.

"Suppose we fill her in," Sabrina suggested, her voice tinged with maliciousness.

At the far end of the table, Claudia's face had turned pale. "Really, Sabrina," she protested. "I

71

hardly consider the Bantry history a suitable topic to bring up over dinner. You know very well Nate has asked us not to discuss it. It's hardly the sort of publicity he wants for the wines."

"Or for himself," Jefferey stated. He glanced reprovingly at Sabrina. "You really can't blame Mother for yielding to Nate's imperial command in this instance. It is a rather unsavory story."

"I had no idea you were so sensitive about your position here, Claudia." Sabrina's voice held a note of cruelty. "Certainly you must have had some idea what you were getting into when you married my uncle. And there is no denying that he was a wealthy man," she added, the impression that I was certain she had intended to convey unavoidable: That Claudia Bantry had married Gain Bantry for his money.

"Not wealthy enough, I am afraid," Jefferey said in his mocking voice, which now held a note of bitterness. "But I am certain that whatever we may have lacked these past miserable years in the way of creature comforts will be more than compensated for when the will is read."

"You are a bit premature in your expectations, aren't you, *Cousin?*" Sabrina said coolly. "I hope you haven't forgotten that I am Gain's only *blood* relative. He was always fond of me. I was like a daughter to him."

"What he wanted was a son," Claudia stated. "He was rabid for a son."

"Which brings us back to Nate," Jefferey said.

He shot his mother an accusing glance. "Why couldn't you have obliged Gain, Mother? Provided him with a flesh-and-blood heir? A snivel-nosed brat would certainly have been a good deal easier to contend with."

"You've heard the rumors in town," Sabrina said. "Now that the seven years of waiting are nearly up, and we've started proceedings to have Gain declared legally dead, they've all been revived. I heard plenty while I was waiting at the hotel for someone to come for me. The general consensus in St. Felicia these days seems to be that Nate is due to inherit everything. Naturally, I wasn't pleased."

"That is impossible," Claudia snapped. "I am Gain's wife and the wife always inherits everything."

"Not necessarily," Sabrina's dark eyes took on a cruel glint. "Delightful thought, isn't it, the three of us destitute, turning to Nate for charity." She turned to me, with a harsh little laugh. "In which case he may very well require your secretarial skills to keep our various accounts straight. It amuses me to think that perhaps that is what he has in mind for you."

"Gain wouldn't have—" Claudia broke off, a look of bitter uncertainty possessing her small features.

"It might be prudent for us all to keep in mind that no one knows for certain—with the exception of his attorney, of course—what Gain saw fit to put into his will. Including Nate. Unless ..." A flash of doubt crossed Sabrina's face.

"Go on, Cousin," Jefferey said.

"Do you suppose it's possible that Gain confided in Nate before he left us? We all know what my uncle was. Unpredictable. An eccentric. And Nate had such a damnable influence over him. I confess there were times when I seethed with jealousy, seeing how close the two of them were. But that is beside the point."

"It could very well account for Nate's Sisyphean efforts to keep up the vineyards, maintain the cellars after a fashion." Jefferey's voice had become objective. It was only when I looked at his eyes that I saw something darkly unreadable stirring in him. "There are other rumors in town," he continued. "Hardly the sort I relish repeating, but I feel that we should be prepared to face whatever comes. What they're saying is that someone murdered Gain. Did away with the body in some clever manner. The perfect crime."

"Nate has been saying that for years, as you very well know," Sabrina said, sounding suddenly bored. "No doubt he is the one who started them."

"But why would he have done a thing like that," Claudia murmured. "It was bad enough, the police poking around."

"Out of spite, perhaps, because we won't go along with his mad passion to keep Vinecroft intact as a productive grape farm. If Gain was murdered, people are going to suspect that one of us here did it. You, Claudia, because he never loved you, and you knew it." Then, when Claudia gasped, Sabrina added sweetly, "I am sorry, dear. But, as Jefferey says, we must face facts. I might have done it because I was jealous of Gain's fondness for Nate. Or even Jefferey, although I can't think of a good motive for you at the moment, darling." She gave Jefferey a quick smile. "It might even have been one of the hands. Sebastian, because his family once was important in this valley and men like Gain took over their lands. There is, of course, yet another possibility. Uncle Gain being the oddball he was, it's just possible that he didn't leave at all. Maybe he's hiding in the cellars and Nate is slipping him his meals. Maybe he and Nate walk at night among the vines. If you recall, they were both fond of midnight strolls."

"Sabrina, for God's sake!" Jefferey seemed genuinely startled by her suggestion. Claudia, I noticed, had turned almost white. "Hasn't it ever occurred to you that the real reason Nate goes about shouting that Gain was murdered is because he did it himself?" Jefferey added bluntly. "Guilty men have strange compulsions."

At the end of the table, Claudia gasped audibly, and a stunned silence fell over us.

I found myself thinking uneasily of Nate Bantry's passionate attachment to the vineyards. Did he *know* that Vinecroft was, by some dark legerdemain, to be his? Was he already anticipating the day when he would gain control of the valuable estate and have a genuine need for a secretary? Was that after all why he had hired me?

I forced myself to visualize Nate as I knew him, recalling his mercurial moods that ran the gamut from warm tenderness to a determined savagery. And found myself unable to deny that such a man might very well be capable of murder.

Chapter Six

While the rest of us were at dinner, Maria had managed to transform the somber library into some semblance of a boudoir. An ancient chaise longue, made up with crisp linens and covered with a bright, turned-back spread, stood invitingly before the bay window, overlooking a broad sweep of lawn. The moon had risen, an immense, silver globe enmeshed in the feathery top of a digger-pine high on the slope, illuminating the endless ranks of vines. Above the vineyards, tangles of wild growth formed an eerie, black pattern over the mountain's silvery shoulders. Somewhere, a coyote yelped, the sound emphasizing the mournful beauty of the colorless landscape.

I remarked on Vinecroft's somber serenity to Maria, who was laying out my things for bed.

My words had a startling effect on her. She came at once to the window, her blasé expression giving way to alarm as she stood searching the shadowed slope.

"What is it?" Her wariness conveyed itself to me and a chill came over me as I recalled Sabrina's odd remark about Gain Bantry.

Was he still alive, as Sabrina had imagined? Did he creep from hiding to move hauntingly over the eerie slopes in the dead of night?

Then, realizing the extent of my own imagination, I brushed the incredible thought aside and said impatiently, "Don't tell me this place has a ghost?"

"Fantasma?" Maria looked at me as though she hadn't quite caught the meaning of my words. Yet I thought, dismayed, she had previously relayed an impression of being as Americanized as I was. I stared up at her puzzled, fancying that I saw a look of cunning lurking in the depths of her black eyes. *"Si!"* she said then, rather quickly. "A ghost! My people call it the Spirit of the Cask."

"Spirit of the Cask?" I remembered the legend Sabrina had mentioned. The thought that there might actually be one seemed slightly preposterous.

Nevertheless, I caught myself peering anxiously past the Mexican girl, into the labyrinth of shadows. Maria reached hurriedly to pull the heavy, sun-streaked drapes. As the dusty cloth swished to close out the night, I saw a movement on the slope above the vineyards. I fancied that it was the hovering, dark form of a man.

Maria had composed herself once more, her face smooth. Unreadable. I assumed that she hadn't seen that illusive figure limned against the moon-dappled night and decided that I had only imagined it. Or if there had been someone, I further assured myself, it was most likely only Nate bent on some obscure, agronomic errand.

Forcing my voice to sound casual, I said, "Tell me about your Spirit of the Cask."

"I'm not permitted to talk about it." Maria's voice was prim. "Now, if there is nothing else I can do for you tonight, I will go."

A sepulchral silence had fallen over the old house, ruffled only by the crisp rustling of the sheets as I snuggled into the makeshift bed. I had the sudden thought that I would be alone on the first floor of the gloomy mansion through the long, dark hours of the night, powerless to escape should there be someone ... something. A chill went through me.

"Where will you sleep?" I demanded of Maria.

"In my own bed as always." Her dark gaze flicked over me, oblivious to my increasing sense of uneasiness. I didn't miss the note of defiance that had come into her voice.

"Would it be possible for you to remain here with me tonight?" I heard my self asking rather desperately.

"Nate didn't ask me to," she said.

"*Mr. Bantry* means something to you, doesn't he?" I regretted the impetuous question instantly, recognizing the pang that had caused me to emphasize his name in a disapproving manner as jealousy.

I had, I realized, become overly possessive of Nate Bantry during the past weeks, simply because he had been kind to me.

"I'm not a fool," Maria said coolly. "I have better sense than to allow myself to care for a Bantry. You needn't concern yourself."

"But I'm only his secretary ..." I broke off, overcome by a belated realization that Maria had very cleverly succeeded in putting me on the defensive. "Beyond that, Nate isn't a Bantry," I added uncomfortably. "Not literally and not that it would make any difference if he were. I've no queer superstitions." It occurred to me then that there was nothing in my experience on which to base ghostly beliefs. Nothing that I could remember. I hadn't *sense* enough to be wary, I thought with a tired sigh, wondering if I would be defending Nate Bantry so avidly if I knew whatever it was that I might have known about him before the accident. "The fact remains that Mr. Bantry was born a Collins the same as Jefferey," I finished lamely.

"Nate doesn't care to be reminded of that," Maria said. "He came to Vinecroft as a child. That is when it all began."

"When what began?"

"The witchery of the vines," Maria said, a hint of the occult vibrating through her soft voice, filling the room with a sense of intrigue. "There is a saying here in the wine country: A true wine-grower is to the cellar born. Even as a child, Nate sought the cellars. The blood of the vines called to him from those cold, dark wombs. Gain Bantry saw that he was different, even then, and he determined to claim him for the vines."

"How do *you* know all of this?" I demanded, appalled by this arcane revelation that seemed to hint at something darkly unnatural about Nate Bantry.

"It is common knowledge here," Maria stated. "My family has always been on this land. I grew up hearing all of the stories. There was something between Gain Bantry and Nate. They were constantly together, man and child. The witchery of the vines," she repeated stubbornly, her words a cabalistic formula, I thought, to Nate Bantry's character. "Only a foolish woman would allow herself to care for a Bantry," she added, her dark gaze dwelling significantly on me. At the same time she gave a little nod toward the drably shrouded windows. "You will find his true mistress out there."

"The ghost you mentioned? Your Spirit of the

Cask?" I blinked at her in horrified astonishment. "But that's utterly fantastic. After all, Nate is flesh and blood."

"I was referring to the vineyards," Maria said. "He lavishes his affection on the vines as though they were his children."

"All of this idle surmise is hinged on the legend, I suppose." Then, boldly, "I suggest that you tell me the whole, wicked tale."

"It's not a pretty story," Maria stated.

I fancied that I caught a promising flicker of conspiracy behind her black eyes, and said, "Jefferey mentioned that fact. Still, if there is some hidden danger I feel entitled to know what it is."

"You will know," Maria stated. "Sooner or later, you will know."

Her obscure words seemed to promise some unexpected and shattering awakening.

Chapter Seven

I lay awake after Maria had gone, attempting to organize the few snatches of information that I had managed to glean since my arrival at Vinecroft. However, fatigue had brought on a gray haze that obscured any rational thought, and I gave up after awhile, becoming aware of the countless, stealthy groanings and creakings that seemed to permeate the outdated mansion.

The lamp that Maria had left burning beside my bed barely touched the chasm of darkness that surrounded me, heavy with the thick, brown smell of old books. I thought how much more pleasant the room would be, filled with the crisp clean rays of moonlight, and slid cautiously from the chaise longue into my wheelchair, wrapping my dressing gown around my shoulders against the chill.

Remembering the impression I'd had of the man's dark form moving among the black shadows, I paused to peer out between the dusty folds before reaching for the raveled drape-pull. The moon hung above the dark shape of the mountain, its illusory, white light spilling over a world that had become a muted study in blacks and whites. There was a faint movement on the broad slope above the vineyards and my heart lurched.

Then the thought struck me that it could very well be a deer weaving its solitary way between the misty clumps of manzanita and wild lilac that glowed luminously in the subtle light, and I gave a relieved little laugh, chiding myself for having allowed the Mexican girl's strange actions to influence me.

High on the ridge, the single coyote that I had

heard earlier had been joined by a chorus. I was overwhelmed by a sudden sense of communion with the magic, half-wild world beyond the dark windows, becoming more firmly convinced than ever that I had, in that illusive time before the accident, known the quiet fruitfulness of vineyards thriving along steep, mysterious slopes. One of the narrow windows that formed the bay had been raised a crack, letting in the lusty smells of damp earth and ripening fruit, blended with the oily, lemon fragrance of the eucalyptus that surrounded the broad lawns.

I lost myself in that undeniably familiar aroma, my gaze still pinned to the section of the mountain where I had seen movement. I knew effortlessly how a deer would look as it emerged from dark shadows, recognizing the impression as a form of memory as the black form detached itself at last to move swiftly across my line of vision.

It was a man, after all, his sinuous body standing out distinctly against a bare patch of moonlight. Nate, I thought uneasily, clad in his slim jeans. Or was it Gain Bantry? My mind asked the incredible question against my will, and I told myself in the next breath that the thought was utterly preposterous. It *had* to be Nate out for one of the midnight strolls Sabrina had mentioned. Alone, I thought positively.

Then, almost as though on cue, a second form appeared, darting to meet the first with quick, lithe movements, reaching, when they met, to

83

blend adroitly into the dark outline of his body. For a shattering instant I imagined it to be Maria's *fantasma*.

Then, as some trick of the light illuminated her bright, print skirt and the glossy darkness of her flowing hair, I realized that it was Maria herself.

I gripped the drapes closed in sickening dismay, the thought coming to me that the girl had deliberately lied. *I know better than to care for a Bantry*, she had told me. Her words echoed through my stunned mind, followed by my own voice insisting that Nate had been born a Collins, the same as Jefferey. I recalled, then, the look of cunning in Maria's eyes, the subtle hint of mockery; and it occurred to me that she hadn't lied after all.

I wheeled myself away from the window thinking that the sullen Mexican girl was even more crafty than I had imagined.

Confusion washed over me in waves. What did Nate Bantry want of *me?* I wondered. Apparently he had no urgent need of me as a secretary, or as a woman. I was able to admit to myself then that I had been harboring a secret hope that the latter might be the case, out of a sense of incompleteness brought about by my loss of memory.

Who was I, then, that he should have taken an interest in me, I wondered rather frantically and rolled myself, in a sudden fit of frustration, to peer into the diamond-shaped mirror that winked at me from the lid of my cosmetic case—another of the expensive accessories that Nate had purchased for me, probably out of the meager funds he had managed to beg from the Old Man Greeves Sabrina had mentioned.

I sat staring at my face, searching for some distinguishing feature.

"Cammy. Cameo Corwin," I said aloud, feeling remote from the girl reflected in the mirror.

Frightened, green eyes stared back at me, above a softly vulnerable mouth that trembled with some half-formed apprehension. I had the sensation that I was dreaming. *Pinch yourself,* a woman's voice said softly out of my past. *Then you will know it is actually happening. You see, dreams do come true.*

The voice held undercurrents of joy mingled inexplicably with sadness. Another voice spoke, my own, *I'm not going to pinch myself. Now the time has come, I don't really want to go.*

Nonsense, the first voice said. *We've waited years for this day. You wouldn't want to disappoint us all. Go, now, darling, and we'll see you soon. . . .*

An inexplicable sense of dread came over me, and the voice trailed off. I realized that I was crying.

I sat alone in the darkly paneled library, gripped by a curious inertia. After awhile, I became aware of the endless ranks of thick, leather-bound tomes marching around me, and knowing that I couldn't simply become a vegetable, that I must make some effort to help myself, I forced my mind to identify them.

Histories. The thought was followed by a slowly dawning realization: The book of mother-lode legends Sabrina had mentioned might very well be among them. Anticipation welled in me and I wheeled myself recklessly toward the high shelves, refusing to admit that my search could very well end in frustration since the majority of the volumes were beyond my reach.

As I began to scan the thick volumes, someone rapped on the library door, calling my name softly through the thick panels. I jerked back with a guilty start, thinking that it was Nate.

But it was Jefferey who stepped into the room, when I called out for him to enter. He closed the door softly behind him.

"You're still up, then." His voice, so much like Nate's, sent a pang through me. "I thought you might be. It's always hard to doze off the first night in a strange place. And I might add that it seemed unlikely that my brother would look in on you with any sort of solace. So I've taken it upon myself."

He came toward me smiling, his eyes intimate.

"I thought I'd read for awhile," I nervously explained my presence in the wheelchair.

"I promise that anything you find on these shelves will be instant anesthesia," he said in that voice that was so poignantly familiar, perhaps because it embodied the few memories I could pin down to a time and place. He scanned the shelves rather intently and I fancied that he had perhaps come to select reading material for himself. Then he said, "I'd forgotten how abysmally dreary this room is. Not a bright jacket among the lot. Would you object too much if I opened the drapes? It's a charming vista outside, all glossed over with moonlight. You really shouldn't miss it." He moved purposefully toward the windows.

"No!" A note of panic sounded in my voice. "Really, I prefer it this way. It's cozier," I added recklessly, unable to put the image of the two people I had seen on the slope from my mind.

Jefferey had turned toward me, a quick excitement burning in his eyes. "I hardly expected—"

I cut him off quickly. "It's just that it's so eerie out there."

His brows lifted. "Don't tell me that damned Mexican wench has been foisting her incredible superstitions onto you," he said. "Nate should have had better sense than to place you in her care. That's it, isn't it? Maria's *fantasma*."

"You know about it, then?"

"How could I help myself, living under the same roof with her?" He gave a wicked chuckle. "And to think that I imagined for a breathless moment that you were inviting me to seduce you. A most pleasing thought since I am almost certain Nate hasn't yet succeeded in overcoming whatever inhibitions you may have."

I flushed furiously. "Please understand, Mr.

87

Collins, that I am here as Nate Bantry's secretary. Nothing else. As for my insistence that the drapes remain closed ... Yes, as a matter of fact Maria did mention some weird phenomenon. Not that I believe in ghosts," I added quickly, wishing that he would go and leave me alone with the questions that haunted me.

No ghost, I thought, could prove to be nearly so dismaying as the confusion in my own mind. I longed suddenly for the comforting fog bank, and knew that it would never return. I had ventured too far into reality to be able to slip back into that comforting oblivion. Whatever came, I was doomed to face it. Doomed. The word echoed chillingly against the frustrating blankness of my mind, and I shivered in spite of myself.

Jefferey came to lean over me, his hands braced on the arms of my wheelchair. "What is it, Cammy?" he demanded. "What did you see out there to make you tremble like that?"

"It was the coyotes, perhaps. They sound so mournful," I said evasively.

He seemed relieved. "I imagined for a moment that you were going to report a sighting," he said, continuing to lean over me, so near that I caught the distinctly masculine fragrance of his hair dressing and cologne. And another, more illusive scent that I tried to identify, and couldn't. Not then.

"Has anyone ever seen it?" I asked. "Maria's Spirit of the Cask?"

"Only Maria, it seems." A shadow passed behind his smile. Displeasure, I thought. With Maria? I wondered. Had she perhaps refused his advances in favor of Nate? Or was he unhappy with *me,* because I had seemed, for a dangerous instant, to promise more than I intended to give? He seemed quite genuinely interested in me, and this flattered me a little.

"What is it?" I asked. "This so-called Spirit of the Cask?"

"You are venturing into hallowed territory, darling, carefully fenced off and guarded by my dear brother. He would hardly approve the turn our conversation seems to have taken. But then he's not here, is he?" A conspiratorial smile fanned upward over his features, crinkling the corners of his eyes devilishly.

I sensed again that Jefferey, for some incalculable reason of his own, was determined to win me, and I suppose I was intrigued by the idea, even excited by it.

I said, "If it is some incredible story out of the past I can't imagine how it can be so important to him."

"You would have to know the story to understand that," Jefferey said.

I hesitated, out of a clinging loyalty to Nate, then said, as I recalled the two figures I had glimpsed in the moonlight, "I feel that I have a certain right to know if I am to stay on here as Nate's secretary."

"You are still deluding yourself," Jefferey said. "In which case I consider it my duty to reveal the scandalous Bantry legend. If you are harboring a secret infatuation for my brother, it may very well serve to open your eyes before it is too late. Nate grew up with the legend. It molded his entire outlook. Surely it has occurred to you by now that he isn't like other men." His words held a dark undercurrent of meaning.

"I hadn't really thought about it," I said, knowing that this wasn't quite the truth, that I *was* perhaps deluding myself just as Jefferey had suggested.

"It's time you did. The whole thing began with the man who founded Vinecroft."

"Gain's father"

"Great grandfather. That first Bantry came west during the gold rush. He'd been a vintner in the East. When he laid eyes on these raw mountains with their thin, gravelly soil, he realized that vines would thrive here. The fact that he had come west in search of gold seems entirely to have slipped his mind."

I said impulsively, " 'Lodes and pockets of earth more precious than the ores, that yield inimitable fragrance and soft fire.' "

The words spilled from the secret realm behind the gray curtain that veiled my mind, startling me almost as much as they did Jefferey.

He gave me a speculative look. "Some of Nate's enthusiasm seems to have rubbed off on you," he said dryly. "I'd no idea you were so taken with these dry hillsides."

"It was only a quotation," I said quickly. "Something I picked up somewhere."

"Robert Louis Stevenson, as a matter of fact. He spent time in this corner of California at one point in his career, penning innumerable, poetic lines which my brother delights in quoting. Another of Nate's idiosyncracies, as you seem to be aware."

"Please go on with the story," I said, confused, wondering if it *had* been Nate who had planted the line from Stevenson in my mind.

"The first Bantry contracted a crew of coolies from a San Francisco Tong and set them to driving cellars into the heart of this damned mountain," Jefferey said. "At the same time, he sent east for cooperage to outfit his winery. There had been a girl he was fond of in Missouri. He'd made some idle promise to her, before he started west. In the meantime, he'd met a saucy California lass who took his fancy, although his Missouri girl friend could hardly have known this, communication being what it was in those days."

"Poor girl," I commented, a sudden vision of the two figures I had seen on the moonlit-slope coming into my mind. "What was her name?"

"Like you, I'm no history buff. I've forgotten, not that it really matters, since she was doomed to tragedy." He gave me a penetrating look and for a stunned instant I fancied that his voice contained a threatening note directed at me.

Then he continued and I realized that he was merely caught up in the drama of the strange story. "When she discovered that cooperage was being shipped to Bantry, out of St. Louis, she very cleverly stowed away in one of the casks, intending to make the long voyage around the Horn to join her lover. However, one of the rough seamen had caught a glimpse of her skirts and she was promptly raped and murdered. Her body was hidden in the very cask that she had chosen to serve as her berth."

"How horrible!" I gasped.

"Yes, it was, rather. Before the ship sailed, that cask, along with the others, was filled with brandy to satiate the thirst of the crew throughout the long voyage and no one the wiser."

I shuddered. "The Spirit of the Cask," I said.

"Exactly. You can see how it might be easy to imagine. But let me finish. It happens that that particular cask was among several set aside for Bantry's personal consumption until his California vintage could mature. Ironically, the girl's body, nicely preserved, was discovered by Bantry himself the night of his wedding to his little California chili pepper. Bantry's new bride was understandably shaken. She is said to have leaped astride her trusty palomino and galloped off into the scrub, never to reappear. . . . A short time later, Bantry took a second bride, a sister to the first. She died after awhile, of pneumonia, I think. It was whispered about, though, that the Missouri girl's unsavory demise had something to do with both the wives' fates and it began to take on the flavor of a curse."

"I can see how it might . . ." I said, forcing down a lingering memory of Maria.

"Especially when you realize that it didn't end there. Bantrys have continued to have bad luck with their women through the years. Tragedy seems inevitable, everything from being tossed off horses to hemorrhaging to death in childbirth. Consequently, it has become a Bantry tradition to marry only for convenience. A cold-blooded way to choose a mate, wouldn't you say?"

"It's unbelievable," I said.

"But that is how it happens to be. And Nate being a Bantry in spirit, if not in the flesh . . . What I am trying to say, Cammy, darling, is this: You really can't expect much of him. None of the more conventional considerations a girl like yourself deserves. If you were to marry him, for instance . . ." Jefferey's brows shot skyward, his green eyes flashing an unspeakable warning.

"Your mother married Gain Bantry and nothing has happened to her," I said.

"Then there *is* more to your coming here than your simply having fallen for Nate's hare-brained scheme about needing a secretary," Jefferey countered.

"I am merely curious about the legend," I said quickly.

"Gain didn't love my mother. Like Nate, he was attached to the vines." A corner of his mouth twisted bitterly. "Theirs was a marriage in the best Bantry tradition, a matter of convenience only. You see, it was only those brides who were loved that met with tragedy."

"I'm sorry. About your mother," I added awkwardly.

"Don't be. I expect Claudia will be well compensated for her patience. It's only a matter of waiting a few more weeks. Gain will be declared dead and we will be free to vacate these dismal premises, begin a bright new life elsewhere."

I had a sudden thought. "I suppose the police looked for a motive when Gain disappeared. Some clue."

"They did what they could. You're already acquainted, of course, with Nate's theory. My brother is a clever man. But then isn't that often the way with eccentrics." Jefferey gave a bitter laugh. "I realize, of course, that you've formed some sort of attachment for him, Cammy darling. But perhaps we can alter that particular illusion. I suggest we try."

The look he gave me seemed to promise a good deal. And although I was fully aware that I couldn't yet trust my judgment of any man, I found myself lying awake after he had gone, trying to imagine what it might be like to belong to him.

Nevertheless, when I dozed off at last, it was Nate who haunted my dreams.

Chapter Eight

I was able, during the next few days at Vinecroft, to put both Maria's *fantasma* and the weird tale that Jefferey had told me from my mind. Jefferey paid a good deal of attention to me, and although I suspected that his attention was prompted at least partially by boredom, it began to seem that life at Vinecroft might be rather pleasant after all.

Then one evening, quite by accident, I came onto the book I had been searching for that first night when he had come to my room. It was hidden high on the shelf, behind a thick volume of Shakespeare that had tempted me to balance precariously on the footrest of my wheelchair in an effort to reach it.

There was no doubt in my mind that someone had deliberately attempted to conceal the book of gold-country legends from me, and my fingers trembled as I flipped open the cover that was protected by a gleaming, nugget-colored jacket. I recalled Jefferey's comment about there being no bright jackets on the shelves and noted that the spine of the jacket was dark. If it *had* been on the shelves that first night, it would hardly have been noticeable among the many thousands of grim books that lined the walls, I thought, thinking too that anyone could have slipped into the library while I was absent to tuck it out of sight.

I began to leaf through it, and an inscription leaped at me from the book's title page, written in a scrawling, feminine hand. *To Nate, who lives the legend; Love always, Sabrina.* A sinking feeling came over me, and I was suddenly aware of how much I had wanted to discredit Jefferey's unflattering implications concerning his brother.

The story I sought was halfway through the book. It was all there, precisely as Jefferey had related it, with a single, shattering addition. The girl who had stowed away in the wine cask had been wearing a brooch when the cask was broken and her body removed. It had been a cameo, with the initials S.H. and C.B. intertwined romantically on its back. The initials, according to the story, stood for Sarah Harding and Caye Bantry, the man who had founded Vinecroft.

The words stunned me and I sat staring blankly at the gray print trying to imagine how that same brooch had come to be in my possession. Only one thing was clear in my mind: In some mysterious way, my own life was intricately linked with the lives at Vinecroft.

When I slid at last into my makeshift bed, still chilled by that numbing thought, I heard the voice again, that same hoarse, whispery cadence that had come to me over the telephone at Jonas E. Gladstone. *Don't remember,* it said this time. *You will be sorry if you do.*

It could have come from anywhere—beyond the shrouded windows, or behind the closed door that led into the gloomy hallway. Or had it come from within myself, because, as Nate had said, I was *afraid* to remember?

I lay listening and when it didn't repeat itself, I relaxed a little, and finally dozed.

Unexpectedly, Nate appeared at breakfast the following morning. He dominated the dismal room effortlessly, an amiable Bacchus smiling across a basket of crisp table grapes that he had just brought in from the coolness of the winery. I was the only one who accepted his offering, choosing an inky cluster of Black Princes that were temptingly elipsoid and as long as my little finger.

"Perhaps I should offer you an olive branch as well," he said. "You do understand, don't you, that it is only because of the vintage that I've neglected you so shamelessly." His amber eyes bored into my own beseechingly, and I found myself responding in spite of the dark doubts I had.

"I had imagined that I might start work before this," I said, certain, for all of the undisciplined throbbing in my chest, that it had been Nate who had attempted to conceal the book of legends from me.

Obviously he hadn't wanted me to know that the cameo brooch that was now in my possession— or had been—had once belonged to Sarah Harding. I remembered how cleverly he had taken it from me, and determined to ask him at the first available opportunity to have it back. Then, if I were wise, I thought, I would find a way to leave Vinecroft.

I became aware of Jefferey's taunting voice saying, "Contrary to the dictates of your monumental ego, Nate, Cammy seems to be faring very nicely without your attention."

Nate glared at him for a suspenseful instant, then turned back to me. "I have a couple of hours free this morning. I thought I might show you the winery, if you're up to it. My office is there."

"*Gain's* office," Claudia protested. "You seem to keep forgetting that it belonged ... belongs to him. You've no right ..."

Nate silenced her with a burning look. "I have every right," he stated. "You know as well as I do that Gain would have wanted me to assume responsibility."

"What Mother was trying to say, before you so

rudely interrupted her, is that you've no right to take outsiders there," Jefferey said. He glanced at me. "Sorry, Cammy. But you *aren't* family. It hardly seems fair that Nate should keep the office door locked to the rest of us, while you apparently are to have access."

"You know damned well why I allow no one in there," Nate said.

"Oh yes. The precious Bantry formularies," Jefferey glanced at me. "Great, moldering ledgers filled with recipes that Nate keeps hidden in a rat-infested hole beneath the office floor. Every wine grower of any consequence has his own secret blends passed down for generations. Another of my brother's pretensions, since Vinecroft is hardly in the running these days. Once the will is read and Claudia disposes of all this, the Bantry formulas won't be worth the mildewed paper they are written on."

"There will always be a Vinecroft," Nate stated chillingly.

"The oracle has spoken, darlings," said Sabrina with a clever little laugh.

At the same time, something that I imagined to be curiosity—or perhaps doubt—slid across her carefully made-up features. I guessed that she was wondering again what Nate might know about Gain Bantry's disappearance and the contents of the will that had become such a controversy in this restless household.

I found that small chink in Sabrina's armor dismaying.

The meal passed on a barrage of barbs and I wondered if it had always been this way at Vinecroft, everyone scratching distrustfully at each other. I was grateful when we had finished and Nate wheeled me out into sunlight.

It was a day to confound the senses and I attempted to lose myself in it, a cowardly urge coming over me to pretend that there were no seething doubts in my own mind concerning Nate Bantry's motives, no hint of ugliness hanging over the big house, with its quaint acres of vines.

My wheelchair rolled smoothly along a gravel path beneath huge, shade trees, with Nate striding competently at the helm. On the far side of the valley, mountains were visible between the ragged, orange-streaked boles of the eucalyptus, their slopes ridged in gray, the live oaks and digger pines forming pools of blue shadow against their pale flanks. A cluster of large, creamy buildings, their red-tiled roofs wavering through the darkness of the trees, stood on the knee of one of the larger hills, and I asked about them, eager to learn all I could about this enchanting countryside.

"The Carmelite convent," Nate said. "We'll visit it when there's time."

"If I am still here," I said.

My chair faltered almost imperceptibly beneath his firm grasp. "Sabrina has been intimidating you," he accused. "Or Claudia with that sharp tongue of hers." Then he drew a sharp breath and my chair came to an abrupt halt on the narrow little path, near a cluster of California poppies that floated over the brown grass like delicate, yellow butterflies. "My God! Not Jefferey! He hasn't been ..." His raging voice broke off sharply. "God help him if he has so much as laid a hand on you," he said then, in deadly tones.

I said quickly, "Jefferey has been marvelous," knowing even as I blurted the words that it was the wrong thing to say to the intense, dark-visaged man on the path behind me.

"Jefferey has a habit of being marvelous when it comes to women," Nate said. "You're to tell me if he gets out of line. I won't have him making passes at you."

"You are very much master here, aren't you," I said.

"Master vintner, at any rate." A touch of lightness had come to his voice and I sensed that he was pleased by my blurted comment.

"So I understand."

"Gain took great pains to teach me that wine-making is a matter of honor and not merely the crushing of grapes and the pasting of labels onto bottles. I've a reputation to uphold."

"You liked your stepfather?" I strained to look up into his bright eyes.

"Liked him?" He flashed me an incredulous

look. "Gain was the only father I ever knew. But then you couldn't have known that, could you?" A perplexing note of expectancy crept into his voice, and I had the sudden, sickening thought that he was trying to trap me into admitting that I had remembered something from before the accident.

"No," I said warily. "No. How could I possibly know anything about you. That is, no more than you may have told me when you hired me to come here as your secretary."

"Gain was a good man. He had honesty. Integrity. He tried to do the right thing. I want you to remember that. Plant it in some corner of your mind, as a start toward an entire new index of memories." His voice seemed to imply that I would be safe as long as I settled for the here and now, refusing to let the past creep back, and I thought how suspicious I had become of him.

At the same time, I felt hopelessly attracted to his vital presence.

We continued along the path in silence, and after awhile he said in a musing voice, "There was a rapport between Gain and me. Something rather special."

"The witchery of the vines," I said, recalling Maria's superstitious comments.

Nate gave me a startled look. "Yes. Something like that, I suppose. I was drawn to this place even as a child. I used to slip up here to hang out in the vineyards and cellars. Surprisingly, Gain didn't mind. He even encouraged my truancy to a degree by offering me sanctuary when Jefferey came poking around searching for me, on Claudia's orders."

"Gain must have been a lonely man."

"There'd been some unhappiness in his past," Nate said.

"There must be some unhappiness in all of our pasts," I said. "I think that it must be unavoidable."

"However, most of us manage to find consolation in one form or another. Gain did, I think. At any rate, it helps to imagine that he did."

"By marrying your mother?" I asked doubtfully, recalling what Jefferey had told me.

"This may sound a bit odd, coming from me. Even a little conceited. But the truth is, Gain married Claudia because of me. You'd have found that out sooner or later, if Sabrina hasn't already told you. I became the son to him that he knew he would never have." He sounded proud of the fact, even a little boastful.

I said, deliberately ignoring the Bantry legend, "I had the idea from somewhere that men marry for love, the same as women."

"I wouldn't know about that." He stopped my chair and stood looking out over the vineyards, his manner evasive. "Gain didn't. Although he had been in love once. A girl named Benita Emery."

"What happened?" I braced myself for another

103

tragedy, thinking at the same time that the legend couldn't be true. There were no such things as curses.

"She went away," Nate said simply, and I drew a relieved breath.

"She didn't love him then," I said.

"Who can say what a woman feels." Nate looked down at me, his mouth lifting mischievously, endearingly, into a sudden, boyish grin. "Cammy," he added softly.

A disconcerting vibration trembled through me. I said quickly, "About Gain . . . If he wanted sons he must have been fond of Jefferey, too."

"Jefferey was beyond salvation," Nate stated. "Toleration of my brother's disinterested presence at Vinecroft was part of the price Gain paid."

"Paid for what?"

"I have just told you. For a son."

I looked up questioningly into his proud face.

"It's very simple, really. Gain wanted to adopt me. But Claudia would have none of it, in spite of the fact that she couldn't provide any sort of decent home for Jefferey and me. My real father had long since walked out on us. The night I was born, as a matter of fact. Claudia was free and she saw her chance to get out of the dirty little tavern where she had worked as a barmaid for as long as I could remember. She hates to be reminded of that period of her life. She wanted to be someone important."

"And so she refused to let Gain adopt you unless he married her," I said, recalling the lines of bitterness in Claudia's small, determined face.

"Something like that. At any rate, Gain took me firmly under his wing."

"While Claudia and Jefferey went their separate ways," I said. "It sounds so . . . cold."

"They had each other. You must have guessed that Jefferey is somewhat older than I am. A dozen years to be exact. He was eighteen when Gain married Claudia. Handsome, with a winning manner when it came to women, and no scruples." He gave me a penetrating look in which I detected a dark flash of warning. "Jefferey wasn't nearly so clever then. He became involved with a girl in town, got her 'in the family way,' to borrow a well-worn euphemism. Her father got in on the show. Brought an unflattering charge against Jefferey. Claudia made it a part of the deal that Gain buy the girl off, pacify her old man with a substantial check. You might say that Claudia used Gain's fondness for me to save Jefferey's neck. To show you the sort of man Gain was, he offered to give Jefferey his name, make him legally a Bantry. It might have helped to erase the scandal. But Jefferey, cocky young fool that he was then, would have none of it."

"Your stepfather must have thought a great deal of you."

"He needed an heir. Someone who felt about the vines and the winery as he did. Not that he didn't provide adequately for Claudia and

105

Jefferey once they were settled here. There was a substantial sum in Claudia's personal account when he disappeared. However, it didn't take Jefferey long to help her squander that nest egg. Jefferey is fond of expensive cars, among other things."

"Sabrina mistook his Mercedes for yours," I said.

"Only because I inherit Jefferey's discards. There won't be any more of those, however. Claudia has bled her account dry. You can see why it would be utter disaster if Vinecroft were to fall into my mother's hands."

"Then you expect to receive at least a share of the estate when the will is read," I ventured, thinking that Nate was no different from the others. It was only his motive that varied.

"I won't deny that I would jump at a chance to lay claim to every inch of this mountainside. The winery. The cellars with their fortune in cooperage." Fierceness possessed his voice, making it harsh. "If Claudia and my doting brother were to get their hands on all of this, not to mention Sabrina who has the homing instincts of a vulture—" He broke off, indicating that the result would be too utterly disastrous to mention. "Sabrina is as eager as any of us to pick Gain's bones, which is her real reason for showing up here at this particular time."

"What a ghastly thing to say!"

"Truth is often unpleasant. Suffice it to say that I fully intend to save Vinecroft."

"How can you, if it goes to Claudia, and, of course, Jefferey, by association. Even Sabrina. They will insist on selling it to be sliced into dozens of expensive tracts." Inexplicably, I felt involved, some part of me rebelling against the idea of all those posh houses smothering the vines, their windows cold, glittering eyes glaring down from the mountainside, destroying its peacefulness.

"I'll find a way," Nate stated.

"You've already had to borrow," I said.

Nate shot me a dark look. "Sabrina's tongue has been wagging again," he said.

"It cost you a good deal to provide care for me at Jonas E. Gladstone. It doesn't seem the sort of thing that an employer would do for his secretary, even if it happened that he needed one." I looked up at him expectantly, wanting desperately for him to explain. Wanting, I thought, my faith in him to be restored.

"Don't worry about it," he said.

His voice was terse, almost to the point of indifference.

Chapter Nine

Nate grasped the handles of my wheelchair and pushed it roughly up the path past a pungent-smelling garden.

Herbs. A sudden nostalgia welled in me, becoming a catalyst, striking memory from the closed, dark surface of my mind like so many bewildering sparks. Fenugreek. Angelica. Blessed thistle. Galingale. I had been intimately familiar with those thaumaturgic herbs, once. There had been a scale, and myself pinching bits of bark and root and seed and dried flowers onto it, watching it sway softly beneath their feather weights. *The art of infusing vermouth is a sort of witchery,* a voice said, out of that indefinite time.

"My new crusher." Nate's voice intruded on it and it receded into the hazy nothingness beyond the gray curtain, leaving me empty. Wondering.

We had come to a gleaming machine standing proudly beside the winery door. Hoses ran from it through openings drilled into the solid, stone walls.

"Must lines," Nate said.

"Yes. I know."

He glanced curiously at me, giving the metal monster a fond pat. "Forty-five hundred dollars' worth of efficiency," he said. "The new must lines cost another thousand. I know it sounds like a good deal of money. But it will have paid for itself in another couple of years."

I had the incredible thought that he was, for some unaccountable reason, intent on justifying the expense to me.

"You sound damnably sure of yourself, Nate." Jefferey emerged suddenly from beyond the thick, rough trunk of the immense live oak that towered over us. "I hope you aren't deluding yourself into believing that you can talk Claudia out of selling, once the will is read."

I wondered uneasily how long Jefferey had been shadowing us, and guessed that Nate must have had the same thought when he said, "What are you doing up here snooping about? Don't tell me that you have decided at this late date to attempt to make yourself useful?"

"Hardly." A look of distaste distorted Jefferey's handsome features. "Except where Cammy is concerned. I wanted to make certain that you didn't go dashing off into the vineyards and leave her stranded." He gave me a conspiratorial look. "The cellars can be frightening, not to mention dangerous. One reason I never venture up here."

"Dangerous?" I said.

"San Francisco's big tremor cracked the back-

109

bone of this entire mountain chain," Jefferey said. "Now don't tell me you haven't read of that particular catastrophe," he added, giving me a peculiar look.

I realized that I had been staring vacantly at him. "I hadn't realized that it affected this area," I said quickly, a vague wisp of memory floating through my mind. "This *is* quite a long way from San Francisco."

Nate, growing impatient, wheeled me abruptly away from Jefferey toward a huge, plank door that, through the years, had weathered to a rich patina.

"You've only to shout loud and clear if you need me, Cammy," Jefferey called after us.

"The personification of chivalry," Nate said scathingly.

"Is it true about the cellars," I asked.

"Jefferey has managed to convince himself that they are unsafe," Nate said. "Salve for his conscience, since he consistently refuses to help out. You'll see for yourself, when we get inside, that the main cellars are perfectly sound. Those that aren't haven't been used for years."

He swung open the winery door and we were swallowed by the cool, moist darkness of the stone building that was like a grotto after the hazy warmth of the path. He wheeled me toward a far corner that had been partitioned off, reaching to take a key from a hiding place between two of the monolithic vats. He seemed not to mind that I

110

watched him curiously and would know where it was kept. This seemed, on his part, to be a gesture of trust and I was touched, the blind faith I had once had in him burgeoning briefly, blotting out doubt.

Then I remembered the legend and his clever confiscation of the cameo brooch, and I became wary again.

The denlike enclosure we entered had retained a certain air of opulence. Turkish lanterns cast a coppery glow over a worn Persian carpet patterned in faded reds and golds. At one end of the room, a teakwood desk stood before a wall banked lavishly with gold medals that attested to the fine quality of the house wines through the years. In one corner, thin-walled tulip-shaped sampling glasses glittered behind the leaded panes of a densely carved armoire.

Nate removed a slim bottle from an outmoded refrigerator that stood incongruously beside the decorative cabinet, and splashed wine expertly into two of the twinkling glasses.

A glow came from the heart of the sparkling wine, and I said, "Sunset in a thundercloud."

"They make poets of us all, the vines." Nate watched me closely, marveling a little, I thought, at my choice of words. "Those of us who have been touched by their magic."

"And you think I have?" I said, feeling slightly guilty as I realized that it had not been my present self who had spoken, but the self I had

111

been before the accident who was now trapped, along with my memories, behind the gray curtain that veiled my mind.

Had her name been Cammy, I wondered idly. Cameo? Like the brooch? And if so, what did it mean?

"I sense a certain rapport between us," Nate was saying.

"Is that why you brought me here?"

"Perhaps." He raised his glass as though to shield his face from me, swirling it slowly, watching the smooth, downward trickle of the dark droplets.

A feeling of fascination came over me, touching some latent chord.

"Les pleurs du vin." It was my other self speaking again, growing impatient behind the gray curtain, stimulated, I thought, by the moist, tangy shadows of the winery.

Had I been here before, I wondered. Was that why it was so familiar to me: the carved armoire with its gleaming glasses; the rows of gold medals marching across the dark wall, and, most of all the heady bouquet that seemed to be all around us.

Nate's eyes had narrowed. "How can you doubt that the magic has touched you?" he said. "You are going to be an invaluable asset to Vinecroft."

"Les pleurs du vin," I repeated. "I'm not even certain what it means."

"It will come to you in time. Don't try to force

it." His eyes had become speculative, and there was a warning note in his voice.

I thought of the warning I had received over the telephone while I was still at Jonas E. Gladstone Memorial. Had it been real, Nate's voice? I found that it frightened me to dwell on it, and took a quick sip from my glass, complimenting him on the flavor of the wine.

"It has potential," Nate agreed. "Beautiful balance. Full bodied, with a delightfully complex bouquet. If I can only afford to hold it long enough . . ." He broke off, a shadow crossing his face. "To develop any kind of name for a house, a vintner has to have the resources to put his wines by for however long it takes for them to attain the peak of their maturity. Unfortunately, I've not been able to do that these past years, and the Bantry label has suffered. For one thing, the floor tax has become prohibitive. One way or another, I've been pressed to move my vintage before it was ready. Regrettably. But only temporarily, thank God. The day is coming, and soon, when Bantry wines will head the list once more. We'll have more gold medals to hang, mark my word." There was an unmistakable ring of confidence in his voice.

When we had finished our wine, Nate wheeled me into the main room of the winery, tucking the office key carefully back into its hiding place. The peculiar sense of awareness that had come over me increased, my heart taking up the whispering

113

cadence of the fermenting vats that towered above us, their systolic and diastolic rumblings as familiar to me as my own breath.

I reached to touch the gummy sugars that had seeped through the thick, redwood staves, knowing even before my fingers came into contact with the tarlike coating how it would feel. The air was redolent with the gases of the fermenting musts. Cabernet. Zinfandel. Sauvignon. Gamay.

An uncanny sense of expectation gripped me and I leaned forward in the wheelchair, searching the narrow catwalks that framed the tops of the tanks high above us for someone who belonged in this mystic setting. Someone out of my past.

For an instant, I envisioned a solitary figure moving wraithlike through the festoon of canvas hoses that twined above our heads like serpents, and I gasped.

"Cammy!" Nate's voice brought me back abruptly to the present. "What is it?"

"I've been here before." I said numbly. "The cameo brooch. . . . You took it from me because it was proof."

"Proof of what?" I twisted in the wheelchair to see him glaring down at me, his eyes burning fiercely out of the shadows. "Proof of what, Cammy?" he repeated mercilessly.

"I don't know," I admitted.

"Who told you about the legend?" he demanded, coming to crouch before me. "Was it Jefferey? Sabrina?"

His intensity frightened me, and I said, "No one," aware that this wasn't the entire truth, attempting in the next breath to pacify my conscience with the thought that Jefferey hadn't mentioned the brooch. There had been no reason for him to, I thought, since he could hardly have been aware that it had been in my possession before Nate so craftily took it from me.

Nate continued to glare at me, and I had the uncomfortable feeling that he could read my mind.

"I found it in a book," I said then. "The book you didn't want me to see. The gift from Sabrina that you hid behind the Shakespeare."

"You must be mistaken about the book being hidden," he said disbelievingly. "No doubt it got shoved in behind the Shakespeare when Carmelita went in to dust. It had to be something like that. To tell you the truth, I'd forgotten all about it."

He brushed the subject of the book aside, but not before I had caught the barest hint of some dark dissatisfaction in his voice.

He continued to crouch before me, his gaze roving deliberately over my features. When I could bear his bold scrutiny no longer, I said, forcing a scathing note into my voice, "I had no idea my face was so interesting."

"Nor I." He drew a deep breath, his mouth quirking into a reluctant smile. Above the white flash of his teeth, a shadow still lurked in his eyes, restless and indefinable.

"The brooch," I said bravely. "I want you to give it back to me."

For a crazy instant, I fancied that he intended to deny all knowledge of it. Then he said, the smile vanishing, leaving his handsome features frozen in a stark grimace of warning, "You'll have it back in good time. For now, forget you ever saw it. Don't mention it to anyone." He reached to take my arms in a steely grasp. "It could very well mean your life, Cammy. Do you understand?"

I cowered from him, tendrils of pain spiraling along my arms. It seemed suddenly that I need only to close my eyes and the protective billows of fog would return to waft me safely away.

I squeezed my eyelids shut and nothing happened. There was only Nate's even breathing and the frightened hammering of my own heart.

Who could I turn to, I wondered. How could I escape the unknown danger that stalked me? I opened my eyes and stared desperately into the dense shadows of the winery, the uncanny conviction that there should be someone there among the huge vats returning to me. Was it Gain I sought, I wondered crazily. Gain Bantry not dead after all?

I jerked free of Nate's impatient grasp, leaning forward urgently in the wheelchair.

"Please!" I cried to that unseen being. "Don't leave me! Don't *die!*"

Then, appalled by the frightening words that

had burst from me with no conscious thought, I slumped dejectedly, overcome by a cruel, aching surety: Whoever it had been was already dead.

Tears burned my cheeks and I buried my face in my hands, desperately willing the fog to come. This time it seemed that it might.

Then suddenly Nate's hands were on my shoulders, shaking me.

"Cammy! For God's sake!" His voice was harsh, dispelling the thin mist that had been there, just beyond my reach.

"Dead," I echoed, a terrible, yawning emptiness hanging over me.

"I know," Nate said softly. His arms came around me and I clung to him, letting him comfort me. "But you still have me, darling. For better or worse, you still have me. Don't ever forget that."

It was only later, after he had wheeled me back to the house, that I remembered his words and wondered what, exactly, he had meant.

Chapter Ten

The fair weather held, the sun gilding the vines by day, the stealthy, coastal fogs seeping through the passes by night to cloak the mountainside in crisp, salty moistness.

"Weather to preserve the bloom," I said, not conscious, until I caught Sabrina's look of amusement, that I had quoted Nate.

"Really, darling, it's bad enough having *one* fanatic wine grower in the house," she quipped.

The four of us, Sabrina, Claudia, Jefferey and myself, were seated on Vinecroft's expansive lawn watching the pickers at work in the vineyards. Nate's men were, for the most part, Mexicans who lived in the row of brown cabins below the dip of the hill during the vintage. One of them, a dark-skinned man named Jesus Estralado, was taller than the rest, slim-hipped, thick shouldered. I hadn't missed the fact that Maria was attracted to him. She had been absent from the house with recurring frequency during the past few days, and more than once I had glimpsed her beside him among the vines. For all of Nate's dark-visaged

118

presence there, I couldn't help thinking, recalling the night I had seen her slipping along the moonlit slope to meet him.

Or had it been Nate waiting there, after all? Perhaps both ghostly figures had been only figments of my imagination. Or *fantasmas*, I thought, remembering how eerie the night had seemed. Caye Bantry and his Spirit of the Cask. Or even Gain. . . .

I broke the fantastic thoughts off, aware that if they continued in that vein they could very well get out of hand. That there was some dark mystery at Vinecroft, I was certain. I was equally certain that it involved me, and I had, during the dark, restless hours spent in the gloomy library, determined to unravel it, once my cast was removed.

I owed it to myself, I thought, to know how the cameo brooch had come to be in my possession. Beyond that, it was unthinkable that I should leave Vinecroft without demanding its return a second time. It had, as I lay awake during the wee hours attempting to organize my thoughts, loomed as a talisman promising me the return of my identity.

Furthermore, I was convinced that Nate Bantry knew a good deal more about me than he had so far revealed, and it seemed imperative that before I left Vinecroft, I should discover exactly why he had taken an interest in me.

As though my teeming thoughts had conjured

him, Nate appeared now out of a cloud of brown dust, riding the topless cab of the rickety truck he used to haul the boxes of ripe fruit to the crusher that waited like a mammoth-jawed monster to devour them, spewing the seeds between iron teeth. His dark head was bared to the sun and the faded work shirt he wore clung darkly to his rippling back. I thought how attractive he was as he passed by, seeming not to notice us.

I had the uncomfortable feeling that for him we didn't exist, that only the vintage was real and worthwhile.

"Damn fool," Jefferey muttered beneath his breath.

"A handsome, damn fool," Sabrina stated.

"My sweet, it must be hell for you not knowing which of us to favor with your considerable charms," Jefferey said. "Will it be Nate? Or me? I can just see indecision gyrating madly through your greedy little mind."

"You are even more of a damned fool than Nate, Jefferey," Sabrina said coolly. "Surely you don't imagine that Gain might actually have left so much as a bottle of his famed Bantry Brut in your name. You must be aware of the fact that he barely tolerated you. If it hadn't been for Nate . . ."

Jefferey cut her off with slim fingers raised in a bored gesture. Only his eyes reflected a deep-seated resentment, their sea-colored depths darkening tumultuously.

120

"Whatever Nate's influence, I don't feel in the least indebted to him," he said. "Anyone who would so blithely relinquish his own father's name in favor of that of a . . ." he gave a mild little laugh. "Let's face it, darling. A *madman*."

"Part of the price Nate paid, darling, for your salvation," Sabrina said. "I know the whole sordid little story. No wonder you despise Nate."

"Sabrina! You're forgetting that Jefferey and Nate are still brothers even though Nate is . . ." Claudia's voice dwindled off as though she couldn't bear to admit whatever it was that she seemed to imagine Nate had become.

"No longer a *Collins*, Aunt?" Sabrina finished for her.

"Gain wanted to make *me* legally a Bantry," Jefferey said. "You were a mere brat at the time, but surely you must have been aware that *I* turned him down. Unlike Nate, I refused to sell out."

"Your nobility shatters me, cousin," Sabrina said. "As I recall, Nate was a mere brat himself, hardly aware that my uncle was a wealthy man."

"Don't kid yourself," Jefferey said rudely. "He was a crafty little bastard even then."

"You *are* jealous of him, aren't you," Sabrina said.

"If this discussion is to continue, I am going inside." Claudia arose abruptly from her chair and hurried off in the direction of the towering old house.

"Sorry, Mother," Jefferey called after her. I saw her small shoulders soften. He glanced at me. "And Cammy. My apologies. It's this damned waiting for Lockridge to set the judicial wheels in motion the instant the seven years are up. Only a few more weeks and that damned will can be taken out of storage. I trust the old goat has kept it safe."

Lockridge. It was the name I had seen in town. He had been Gain's attorney then, I thought, pleased that I had been able to place it.

"Everyone but Nate is on pins and needles," Sabrina said. "I marvel at the way he plods patiently on, so completely wrapped up in the vines that nothing else seems to matter."

"I've a suspicion that you intend to remind him of your presence here," Jefferey said knowingly. "Which leaves Cammy and me to our own designs, an idea that I find rather pleasing." He shot Sabrina a taunting look.

"If you are trying to be clever, Jefferey, I fail to get the point," she said coolly. She turned to me. "I'm going inside. I'll send Maria to rescue you if you like."

"I *am* rather tired," I said, suddenly eager to get away from Jefferey who was watching me with a smile that reminded me of a cat toying with a mouse.

The old house seemed more dismal than ever after the bright sunlight outside, and I tried to think of ways to amuse myself, rejecting the tiers of books with a single glance.

Beyond the bay window, I glimpsed Jefferey striking off along one of the dusty lanes that circled the vineyards, walking swiftly, his head down.

Behind me, Maria said, "It's a nice day for a walk."

"Nate mentioned that Jefferey enjoys fast cars," I said. "Yet he never seems to leave the farm. He must be more attached to Vinecroft than he would like to admit."

"His car is needed here now," Maria said obliquely.

"But no one uses it. That is, not often," I added, recalling having seen Claudia and Sabrina driving off once or twice in the shining Mercedes.

"It is the only car on the farm and we are some distance from town," Maria explained. "During the vintage, emergencies sometimes arise, and the truck isn't licensed for use on public roads. Nate cuts expenses where he can."

And yet he had taken over my life at great expense to himself, I couldn't help thinking. I said, "I understood that Nate had his own car. Jefferey's cast-off, was the way he put it. A Mercedes, I assumed."

"It is in town for repairs," Maria said.

Her words held no significance for me then, and I said, "I'd like to go back outside if you don't mind. This old house is too gloomy for words. To the winery," I added on impulse.

Maria gave me a suspicious glance and I guessed that she imagined I wanted to waylay Nate.

"I haven't yet been inside the cellars," I said quickly, suddenly aware that something of the sort *had* been in my mind.

There was no sign of him, however, when we reached the huge, stone building thrusting out of the hillside. I urged Maria to wheel me inside and she obeyed reluctantly, maneuvering my chair skillfully over the canvas lines laced between the huge vats.

The same sense of expectancy I had experienced the day Nate had brought me to the winery flooded through me, and I insisted that she wheel me deeper into the moist darkness. The dense shadows closed around us, more impenetrable than ever, refusing to yield whatever tenuous secrets they held.

The black mouth of a cave yawned in the wall ahead, a light switch beside it, its bare wires frayed dangerously against the damp, stone wall. I reached cautiously to flick it and bare bulbs glowed feebly, lighting a dingy, vaulted corridor that had immense, oval-shaped casks racked along either side. There was something incredibly familiar about it and I asked Maria to wheel me deeper into the mountain.

The huge casks seemed almost to glow with

some evil, dark light and I realized how deeply affected I had been by the story of Sarah Harding's horrifying demise. If the casks glowed it was only because their richly carved heads were varnished to a high luster, I told myself sensibly, taking deliberate stock of the long tunnel.

Above our heads, the ceiling was furry with some dark, pungent mildew.

"Wine loss," I said unthinkingly.

Then wondered, as Maria gave me a startled look, how I had known that. It was eerie discovering things about myself that I couldn't consciously remember. If I remembered wine loss, I reasoned, I had apparently been in a wine cellar before, and I wondered again if I might have had that experience here at Vinecroft. It hardly seemed likely, since none of the occupants of the old house had seemed to recognize me upon my arrival. Still, the feeling persisted that I had once been intimately involved with wine growing.

"We'd better turn back now," Maria said, interrupting my idle musings.

The Mexican girl seemed suddenly to be afraid, her hands becoming tense on the handles of the wheelchair. I guessed that she too had recalled the strange story of Sarah Harding.

"Now that I am here I want to see all of the cellars," I insisted.

"The *fantasma*," Maria said softly, an eerie note coming into her voice.

"I know all about your Spirit of the Cask," I
125

said, stifling a little chill. "She was simply an unfortunate girl in love with the wrong man. I assure you that if your ghost does exist I'm not frightened of her."

Surprisingly, my words contained a ring of truth. I had come to feel a sense of kinship with the long-dead Sarah because of the brooch. It occurred to me then that her body might very well have been secreted in one of the very casks racked before me and I gave an involuntary shudder, at the same time demanding that the reluctant Maria wheel me deeper into the cellar.

"As you say," Maria replied, something coming into her voice that I failed to identify. Not fear, I thought, but some furtive emotion. Cunning? The word came to me unexpectedly.

We passed by the yawning, black mouths of yet more caves beehiving the heart of the mountain, several of them blocked with crisscrossed planks heavily coated with wine loss. The *dangerous* cellars Jefferey had mentioned, I thought.

Then Maria swerved my chair sharply to the left into yet another tunnel, its vaulted ceiling still bearing the marks of the chisels used by the Chinese laborers to hollow it into the solid limestone. Rows of black casks marched away from us and the pungent smells of the vintage were everywhere.

The only sound was the soft swishing made by the wheelchair's narrow, rubber tires on the moist floor as Maria pushed it rapidly ahead, seeming determined now to show me every last inch of the meandering cellars, swerving my chair into yet another of the yawning caves. Bare bulbs dangled from moldy wires over our heads, the majority of them burned out here, those that still burned casting an inadequate gray light through their coating of wine loss.

The casks racked in this section of the cellar were smaller, more closely crowded together. Stags, I thought. *Handmade cooperage growing more precious with age, like old violins. . . .* Someone had said that to me once. Or had I read it somewhere? I closed my eyes and tried to concentrate.

Maria had brought my wheelchair to a halt before one of the pungent-smelling casks, the trap on this one standing open, revealing the thick coating of cream of tartar inside. Ahead of us, yet another of the boarded-up tunnels opened off between the crowded racks.

I became suddenly aware of a sound issuing from it, faint at first, then growing in volume. I sat paralyzed, knowing even before the words came, what it was.

"Don't try to remember." The dreaded voice vibrated around me, muted, rasping out an unspeakable threat. "If you do, you will drown in the wine. The red wine seeping like blood into the cask. Do you understand me, *Cameo?*"

I sat numbed by a chilling sense of unreality, the dimly lit cave whirling around me.

127

"Don't remember!" The ominous words came to me faintly, then faded away into nothingness.

Had they been real? Gain Bantry, perhaps, hiding in the boarded-off cave for some unspeakable reason, just as Sabrina had suspected? Or had it been the Spirit of the Cask?

But that was incredible. I drew a deep breath, driving out the wild thoughts, thinking that I must remain sensible. Not panic.

When the room had stopped spinning, I turned to Maria. Only to find that the Mexican girl had fled.

I was alone in the horrifying, dark tunnel.

"Maria!" A note of terror shrilled in my voice. I paused to listen for a breathless moment, fancying that I heard her running footsteps echoing from beyond one of the sharp turns in the beehiving cellar. "Maria! Come back here! Don't leave me."

Somewhere, very softly, someone gave a mad, cruel laugh.

I clutched my hand over my mouth to keep from crying out, feeling fear crawl along my spine with cold, insidious fingers. Then cried out again for Maria.

There was only the sound of my terror echoing along the cold, stone walls.

Frantically, I jerked at the chrome wheels of the chair, sending it lunging recklessly between the casks, past the carelessly boarded opening that harbored whoever ... whatever it was that had threatened me. A black mouth yawned on my right, and another. I maneuvered my chair into the dark opening, turning it around, wheeling it desperately back along the endless corridor.

There were too many of the yawning cellars. Confusion overwhelmed me as I tried to decide which way we had come. There had been a chain of the naked, gray-scummed bulbs lighting the way. Now there were only yawning, black mouths opened to swallow me. Someone had flicked off the lights, I thought; someone determined to frighten me; someone real who knew that my name was Cameo.

Nate? His name was like a wound in my mind. I suddenly remembered the look of cunning that I had caught on Maria's face and thought: The two of them are conspiring against me in some sly scheme.

Then without warning the remainder of the lights flicked off and I was plunged into a chasm of darkness more terrifying than anything I had ever known.

"Don't remember!" The voice repeated itself over and over again in my mind.

Or was it real, moving nearer to me through the thick blanket of darkness that seemed almost tangible in its density?

There was a sound behind me, someone moving through the caves. I heard the scrape of shoe leather on rough stone. The footsteps came nearer. As abruptly as they had gone off the lights came on again and I turned in my chair to see a faceless, dark form bearing down on me.

Terror gurgled in my throat and I clutched madly at the wheels of my chair, sending it crashing among the casks that crouched around me like hunchbacked beasts on their shallow racks.

I managed to right it at last and sent it plunging along the dimly lit passageway that narrowed suddenly, the floor becoming strewn with rubble. Somewhere I had taken a wrong turning. Crisscrossed planks loomed before me, and I knew then that I was trapped.

"Cammy!" The faceless form closed in on me. Unbelievably, it had Nate's voice.

I tried once more to send my chair ahead. The wheels caught on a rotting stave and it jerked sideways, striking the limestone wall. A patter of loose stone showered from somewhere above me.

"Cammy!" Nate's voice called to me out of that frightening faceless being.

I screamed. Then something unyielding thudded onto my head and the world folded around me.

I was lost in darkness.

Chapter Eleven

"Cammy! Open your eyes, for God's sake! Look at me!" The voice was insistent, penetrating the shroud of darkness that pulsated around me on waves of pain.

Nate's voice. I shrank from it as recognition came.

"Cammy! It's all right. It's me." Strong arms braced me and I realized that I was sitting in my wheelchair.

Gradually, as awareness returned, I remembered where I was and what had happened. In spite of the cruel voice warning me, I was still alive, I thought hazily. The arms encircling me felt safe and shielding.

"Jefferey," I said, opening my eyes.

The person who held me had no face. I uttered a terrified cry, then realized that he was wearing some sort of mask. He pulled the heavily screened headpiece away from his face and I saw that it wasn't Jefferey after all, but Nate.

"I hope you aren't too disappointed," he said in a voice tinged with bitterness. "After all, this is hardly Jefferey's domain. I've been turning champagne magnums in the depths of the cellar. The mask is my protection against exploding bottles."

In the depths of the cellar. . . . The whispering voice had come from the depths of the cellar, I couldn't help thinking as I looked up numbly into his weathered face. I raised my hand to touch my aching head and it came away smeared with something darkly wet and viscous. Blood.

"You tried to kill me," I accused. "Why? Why are you so frightened of whatever it is I might remember?"

"You're hurt!" He seemed surprised. "I thought you'd only slipped off again, as you used to do at the hospital. I was warned that it could happen. I hoped it wouldn't."

I wanted to believe him and couldn't because of the blood. I said, "What are you going to do to me?"

He was kneeling to examine the floor and now held up a small boulder. "Look," he said, ignoring my tremulous question. "A rock came loose and bounced off your head. That's all there is to it. It was a small one, thank God." He arose to examine my bleeding scalp. "It's only a slight abrasion. Head wounds always bleed more profusely than the injury seems to warrant. It's nothing, really. The ache should go away in a few minutes, and you'll be back to—" He broke off and I guessed that he had been going to use the word *normal* and had thought better of it. "You shouldn't have come in here alone, you know. Not until you've learned your way about."

"I wasn't alone," I said. "Maria was with me. She disappeared. As if you didn't know," I added, some stubborn part of me refusing to trust him.

"What is that supposed to mean?"

"She slipped away while I was distracted by the voice." I said recklessly. "The same voice that came to me over the telephone while I was at Jonas E. Gladstone Memorial. *Your* voice," I accused hysterically. "You don't want me to remember. You've made that clear to me from the beginning. There's really no need for you to threaten me in such an abominable manner. I shall go away quietly. Just give me back my brooch and I shall ask Jefferey to drive me into the city." My voice had risen to an unflattering pitch.

Nate gripped my shoulders fiercely. "Are you out of your mind?" Then, realizing what he had said, he shook his head angrily. "My God! I didn't mean that. Listen to me, Cammy. This crazy notion you've got about hearing voices. . . . Dr. Simmons, pedantic little pedagogue that he was, explained to you exactly how it would be. The snatches of memory coming at odd moments. . . . If you heard anything it had to be out of your past, some half-remembered snatch of conversation erupting out of your own mind. You can't expect all of your memories to be pleasant ones. Not under the circumstances."

"You mean because I tried to kill myself."

"Attractive young ladies don't go about throwing themselves over cliffs for no reason," he said, his voice softening a little. "Be reasonable, darling—"

"There *was* a voice," I insisted, cutting him off. "Maria heard it too. Why else should she have gone off and left me alone? I know all about you and Maria. You had some sort of plan—" I broke off abruptly on a sudden note of defeat, realizing that what I said hadn't quite made sense.

"Dammit, Cammy. Listen to me. There was no voice. And I haven't seen Maria. Not today, at any rate." His qualification of the statement seemed to shield guilt of some sort; some shameful involvement that I didn't want to think about. "When I do see her, I fully intend to give her hell for running out on you like this. No doubt she saw her chance to slip off and join Jesus. But enough of idle conjecture. Let's get you out of here. Your hands are like ice."

He grasped the handles of my wheelchair and turned it about.

"This is one of the cellars that collapsed during the 1906 tremor," he said, making casual conversation, trying to divert me, I thought, from the voice. "My grandfather lost a fortune in cooperage and wine."

"Your adopted grandfather, don't you mean?"

He gave a queer little laugh. "Of course. I sometimes forget that I wasn't born a Bantry. My God, but they had an exciting life. Gain told me

134

that wine flowed out of this mountain in rivers during that awful quake. Barrels and bottles bouncing along on eight feet of blood-red medium. The vineyards below were bathed in it. Maybe that's why they consistently produce a rare vintage."

"In spite of the Spirit of the Cask," I murmured.

Nate stopped my chair to give me a startled look. "The Spirit of the Cask? For God's sake, where did you come up with a notion like that?"

"Sarah Harding's ghost," I said. "Maria told me that is what it is called."

"This is the first I've heard of it," Nate said.

I saw skepticism in his eyes, seeming to insinuate that I had made the whole thing up. I thought again how clever he was. He and Maria.

We had emerged from the dank gloom of the cellars and the winery, into the vivid, warm sunlight.

"I can make my way back to the house from here," I said, taking a firm grip on the chrome wheels.

"You still don't believe me about the voice," Nate said. "I won't let you go until you realize that no one wants to frighten you. Least of all me." He posed himself before me, determined that I should see things his way.

The mask, when he had torn it free, had ruffled his hair into glossy little points so that he became a dark-visaged satyr leaning over my chair. A flame leaped behind his eyes, seeming in some uncanny way to illuminate the smooth planes of his face. The smell of sulfur clung to him from the vines, blending into the aroma of wine and tobacco and the smooth, clean scent of his skin. None of it seemed quite real and his claret-steeped features floated before me, threatening to spin away into nothingness.

Was any of it real? I wondered crazily. Nate? Vinecroft? The cameo brooch and the voice that I thought I'd heard. Or was it all part of some fantastic dream? Would I suddenly awaken to find that everything had disappeared? If that happened, where would I find myself? Who would I be?

I felt like a dandelion tuft scattered by wind, my thoughts dancing off wildly in all directions.

Then suddenly Nate's lips were pressing my own, drawing me back together again and I clung to him, feeling the warm tautness of his flesh, thinking crazily that real or not he was all I had.

Chapter Twelve

The day finally arrived when my cast was removed by a kindly doctor in St. Felicia who had,

Nate informed me, been caring for Bantrys for years. I would have to favor my ankle for awhile, the doctor warned me. Otherwise I was free to come and go as I pleased.

It was the vineyards that held the greatest attraction for me. I walked often among the vines, gradually increasing the length of my strolls as my ankle strengthened. Indian summer possessed the hillsides in all of its gold and bronze glory and the air was hazed with smoke rising from the bonfires on the valley floor. The fragrance of burning leaves combined headily with the redolence of the fermenting musts and tingly young wines that Nate watched over with unwavering devotion.

I seldom saw Nate those days. Yet I had grown more acutely aware than ever of his mercurial presence. I knew that he had stopped smoking and had given up sweets and spices. I knew too that he had begun tasting and classifying his precious new vintage and that it was for this reason that he denied himself, honing his senses to razor-keenness. His entire being had become concentrated unalterably on the wines, I thought. With the exception of his midnight excursions with Maria. . . . Unwillingly I recalled the one or two fleeting glimpses I'd had, since that first night, of someone moving stealthily along the slope above the vineyards.

If I had believed in the supernatural I might have been able to convince myself that there were such things as *fantasmas*. As it was, I knew the forms I saw moving about in the dark shadows of night to be only too real, even though midnight excursions seemed at variance with the dedicated person Nate had become during the busy days of the vintage. He had, as Sabrina put it, become fanatical about the wines. Still, he was undeniably male, and there was a certain sleekly clad litheness about the figure I had glimpsed on the moonlit slope that convinced me that it was Nate.

His complexities served only to make me the more fascinated by him, and I told myself as I walked among the Zinfandels and scraggly Pinots that, as much as I felt drawn to Vinecroft, the time had come for me to leave. Nate could hardly stop me, I reasoned, in spite of the fact that he had in some incalculable way managed to have himself declared my guardian.

I had gone so far as to answer several newspaper ads placed by firms requiring the services of an able secretary. So far, my attempt to find employment in this rather distant manner had proved fruitless, and I comforted myself with the thought that I couldn't very well go without my brooch, or without knowing what part Vinecroft had played in my life before the accident that had so efficiently wiped out my memory.

It didn't occur to me then that I was seeking excuses to remain near Nate. The truth is that I had fallen madly in love with him and the hint of wickedness I saw in him seemed only to enhance the feeling.

It was Jefferey who seemed most intent on winning me. And although I considered him an attractive man for all of the incomprehensible hint of intrigue that I often glimpsed moving behind his storm-colored eyes, that certain magic that Nate's mere presence could arouse in me was missing.

I wondered this day, as I struck off up the slope, where it could possibly end. Lost in my own thoughts, I didn't realize, until I had come upon the clump of shadowy live oaks, that I had followed the course taken by the two elusive figures I had glimpsed that first night coming together in the moonlight.

Overcome by a sudden thrust of distaste, I turned abruptly to gaze out over the vineyards, letting their quiet orderliness soothe me. Gradually as I stood there, a creeping sense of uneasiness came over me. The hairs on the back of my neck prickled, and I knew instinctively that I was being watched.

At the same time a twig crackled somewhere above me and I spun quickly about, careless of my weak ankle, feeling it wobble beneath me, sending a flash of pain running up my shin.

Stalked. The isolated word whipped through the dark curtain that veiled my memory and I knew unerringly that, in that inaccessible period of time before the accident, *I had* been followed by something; someone whose presence had chilled me. Someone from Vinecroft, I thought

139

wildly, as an indefinable sense of fear overtook me; thinking too that there *had* been a voice, for all of Nate's fierce insistence that I had only imagined it.

I searched the steep slope above me frantically for some threatening movement, not knowing what to expect, knowing only that I was in danger. The live oaks climbed innocently above me, blending into the feathery shadows of digger pines that gave way higher up to a spiny jutting of limestone.

Overhead a hawk soared on spread wings, and somewhere in all of that benign stillness someone crouched, as stealthily cunning as the wild animals that roamed the tawny slopes by night, emitting their untamed cries.

If I had been brave perhaps I might have made my way up the hill and ferreted out whoever was there waiting to spring. Instead, I stood paralyzed by a chilling fear, thinking that it could be any one of them. Nate. Jefferey. Claudia. Even Sabrina, who made no effort to hide her disapproval of the attentions Jefferey paid to me. Or Gain. . . .

Had Nate's stepfather truly been a madman, as Jefferey insisted on believing? I wondered. Had his queerness prompted him to conceal himself in some hidden corner of the dank cellars to become a hermit who roved abroad only in secret? Had I once known him?

I turned, suddenly fearful of memory itself, and plunged recklessly into the vines, feeling their bronzed fronds close around me like safe, sheltering arms.

"*Perdon*," a voice said nearby, and Sebastian rose from between the vines of the next row, the shears he used to gather grapes gleaming in his hand.

I uttered a wild little cry.

"I didn't mean to frighten you," he said, tucking the scissors that had seemed, for a paralyzing instant, to threaten into his wide, leather belt.

"There is someone up there," I blurted, pointing up the slope.

Or had it been Sebastian's eyes I had felt, peering at me from between the vines?

The small, brown man squinted up the hill. "I see no one, *Senorita*." I couldn't help thinking that the Spanish title seemed slightly incongruous coupled with his perfect English, as had Maria's *fantasma*.

"Nevertheless, I am certain there was someone. Spying on me," I added impulsively.

Sebastian gave me a piercing look, his black eyes burning between leathery lids. "In that case, it would be well to remain near the house," he said. "You resemble someone who once came here. I have seen the likeness. And if I have seen it, there are others who might see it as well."

I gave him a bewildered look. "Who is it I resemble?"

He hesitated, his birdlike eyes scanning my

face as though he were attempting to read my thoughts, then said, "Nate hasn't told you?"

I shook my head.

"I have spoken out of turn. It is nothing, I assure you. She has been gone a long while."

"Maria's *fantasma*?" I said disbelievingly.

Sebastian gave me a blank look. "What has my daughter been telling you?"

"About a ghost," I said.

"I have told her too many stories," he said. "Caye Bantry's unfortunate brides were members of our family. The Revis-Gerara household was one of the most noble in California in those days." He shrugged. "*Si*. But look at us now. However, it has been good caring for the vines. They are my life, just as they are Nate's. We are *simpatico*. But a young girl needs more than that. She needs romance. I have tried to provide it with my stories of the past. Is it any wonder Maria speaks to you of ghosts?"

"I think I should know, if I resemble someone," I began.

Sebastian shrugged off my words. "It is nothing," he said. "My imagination is great. It is nothing."

With that, he hurried off, leaving me staring after him more puzzled than ever. I could wait no longer, I thought. I had to uncover the significance of the cameo brooch and Nate's real reason for bringing me to Vinecroft.

142

That same night I set out boldly to explore Nate's office. It seemed reasonable to assume that any evidence there might be linking my life to the lives of those at Vinecroft could very well be secreted in the denlike room that had once belonged to Gain Bantry. I wondered why that possibility hadn't occurred to me sooner and knew that it was because I had felt helpless and afraid.

I was still afraid. But now that I could get about without the wheelchair I could afford to ignore the apprehension that gripped me, sending icy fingers along my spine as I crept out into the cool, moist night.

I slipped furtively through the inky shadows cast by the towering eucalyptus, not yet daring to snap on my light. I reached the winery at last, only to discover that someone was there before me. Light glowed softly through the single window that had been set into the partition separating the small enclosure from the noisy aerations of the vat room.

I peered cautiously through the small, encrusted panes and saw that the worn Persian carpet had been rolled back to disclose a trapdoor that stood open above a darkly yawning crypt. The "rat-infested hole" Jefferey had mentioned, where the formularies were kept.

A moment later, Nate's dark head appeared above the plank floor, as he climbed out of the uninviting pit, slamming the heavy door down behind him, flipping a hasp into place which he secured with an ornate padlock.

There had to be a key, I thought craftily, my heart thudding with the knowledge that Nate might very well, in his fine-honed keenness, sense my presence. Still I dared to watch breathlessly as he removed the key I had hoped for from his jeans' pocket and went to open the center drawer of the teakwood desk. He fumbled inside it for an instant, his fingers prying into some secret niche. When he removed his hand, the key was gone.

The door to the office opened at last and I pressed myself against the dark stickiness of one of the mammoth tanks, grateful for the vibration of the huge vats that drowned out the frightened hammering of my heart.

I waited for a long while after Nate had gone before I finally dared to take the key from its hiding place and open the door of the office. It was another eon before I dared to turn on one of the Turkish lamps.

I went at once to examine the center drawer of the desk, the eerie presence of a crypt suggesting that anything I might hope to find would be hidden there. A tiny panel at the back of the drawer sprang open beneath my touch and I removed the second key, my heart beating more wildly than ever.

The crypt, when I had managed to roll back the rug and lift the heavy door, was even more formidable than I had imagined. I drew a deep, steadying breath and descended bravely, flashing my light downward to illuminate the steep, narrow steps.

Dusty bottles were racked along the walls of the square, stone-walled enclosure. Nate's most precious vintage, I thought. Zinfandel. Barbera. Mourestel. The names on the bold labels struck a familiar chord.

An outdated safe, elaborately scrolled in gold leaf, dominated one moldy corner of the small room, its thick door standing wide, its interior dismayingly empty. Above it, rows of leather-bound journals leaned along dusty, plank shelves, their covers mildewed and curling. The formularies Jefferey had mentioned. One of them contained a white marker and I reached to take it down.

The slip of paper marked the blending recipe for the house's famed Bantry Brut, the directions written in copperplate, the complicated swirls long since faded to a dusty brown. I visualized Nate secreted in the cool darkness of the crypt, his dark head bent intently over the ancient journals as he meticulously memorized the instructions that would perpetuate the house's mark and brand, and thought again how complex he was. How far beyond my understanding.

I turned the page, scanning another of the carefully written recipes, this one setting forth the rules for infusing vermouth. *Keep vermouth true to type. Allow no one flavor to overpower the*

145

rest. Stay true to the house. . . . Had Caye Bantry penned those instructions, I wondered. Had the vines possessed him as they did Nate? Was that why he had forgotten whatever promise he had made to Sarah Harding?

The legend seemed suddenly real to me as I sat staring at the faded copperplate, and I visualized Sarah Harding, vitally alive, her eyes sparkling with the daring of her adventure as she hid inside the mammoth oval cask, not realizing that it was to be her coffin. The cameo brooch would have been pinned to her collar, I thought, just as it had been pinned to my own.

The comparison sent a queer feeling of dread through me. Had Sebastian Revis-Gerara imagined that I resembled the dead girl's ghost, I wondered crazily. Was I doomed to die just as Sarah had been? Did the cameo brooch carry a curse?

I closed the heavy formulary with a resounding thud and reached to shove it back onto the dusty shelf, thinking that I must get away from this place. I must run.

Unexpectedly, an envelope fluttered from between the old journal's warped pages and landed at my feet. Distracted from my frightened thoughts, I bent to retrieve it and saw that it was addressed to Gain Bantry, in a delicately feminine hand. It had a San Francisco postmark, dated twenty years earlier. The small, smeared numerals seemed somehow significant and my hands began to tremble with some half-defined premonition as I guiltily slipped the folded pages from the yellowed packet.

I suppose I knew, even before I began to read, that the contents of the envelope somehow concerned me.

There was a receipt folded inside the letter dated only a few weeks earlier and made out to Nate. The name William J. Cassidy was printed boldly across the top of the form and beneath it, in more modest letters, the dismaying words, Private Investigator.

Numbly, I forced myself to read the small, feminine script that covered the blue pages of the letter.

"*My darling Gain,*" it began. "*I have done an abominable thing. Please forgive me. I am not trying to make excuses for myself. I merely wish to explain to you why I have done this terrible thing. I want you to understand, if you can, that under the circumstances I had no choice.*

"*It hasn't been easy for me since I left St. Felicia. Many times I have thought of writing to let you know that I didn't leave there alone. I was carrying your child when I went away. Knowing the sort of man you are, I considered more than once using her to bring you to me. To force you into marriage. How utterly distasteful that seems to me, even now, which is perhaps why I could never quite bring myself to do it. I wanted you to come to me because you needed me. Loved me.*

Any other way would have been defeat, for both of us. You had to be the one. . . .

"But why dwell on that now. What is done is done. I have abandoned your child. I had no choice. I am quite ill and was unable to care for her. I have been discreet in what I have done. There was no doctor present when she was born. No one. I bore her alone and went with her, when I was strong enough, to the steps of St. Joseph's in the Little City. Perhaps you have discovered by now that the cameo brooch is missing from the jewelry box in the room where they laid out the girl from the cask. I have no idea why I took it. Perhaps I had some idea that it might remove the curse that seems to have held all Bantrys in its grip since that long-ago tragedy, and you would realize that no harm would come to me if we were to marry. You see, Sebastian told me all about your fearsome legend. He is very good at telling stories and of course I believed all of the wild tales he spun for me when I went into the vineyards with him to gather grapes for the table. Those were happy days, those days I spent with you at Vinecroft. . . .

"But to get back to my own story. You didn't come to me as I had hoped, and now it seems propitious that they forgot to pin the brooch to Sarah Harding's dress when they laid her away. It was the only thing I owned with which to identify your child for you, in the event that you might want to come to the city and claim her. It is

148

*pinned to her blanket. The Sisters will undoubt-
edly take her to the foundling home. I rest assured that you will find her there, if it is your
wish.*

*"The sand in the hourglass is running out for
me. I will be gone by the time you hold this
letter in your hands."*

The name at the bottom of the page was Benita. Benita Emery, the girl Nate had mentioned so
casually to me. The girl that he had said Gain
Bantry once loved.

Comprehension pried tentatively at my
numbed brain. *I* was that abandoned child with
the cameo brooch pinned to her blanket, I
thought. *I* was Gain Bantry's daughter!

The letter seemed suddenly to burn my fingers
and I reached for the formulary, clawing numbly
at the crinkled pages in my eagerness to slip it
between them, out of sight. As I did so, a newspaper clipping fell from between them. CAMEO
GIRL FOUND NEAR DEATH. The caption
leaped at me. Stunned, I stared at it for a long
while before I could bring myself to read the
short article.

The story of my rescue by the skin divers was
precisely as Nate had described it. Except, I
noted numbly, that there was no mention of attempted suicide. There was a brief mention of
the initials engraved on the back of the brooch.
According to the newspaper article, they were
G.S. and H.B. There were several spelling errors

149

in that particular paragraph and I realized that the strange initials were a misprint.

This then, I thought, was why no one else had come forward to identify me. Only Nate had realized who I was. And even he had made doubly certain by hiring a private investigator to trace me.

The thought chilled me, and I ran up the steep stair and slammed the trapdoor closed behind me as though I could seal in the dark doubts that haunted me.

Outside, a lopsided moon hung over the mountains, illuminating the vines. I ran toward them, a throng of unanswerable questions swarming through my mind. Had Gain Bantry—my father—found me? Had I lived at Vinecroft at some time in the past? Was that why Nate Bantry had brought me here?

I stumbled blindly along the dusty hillside, not realizing until a straggling arm of dead manzanita reached to grasp me that I had left the vines behind. The slope rose above me, shrouded in unspeakable mystery. I had come much farther than I had realized, driven on by the questions that pounded relentlessly through my mind.

Why? Why?

I began to run, ignoring the dull ache that had sprung up in my weak ankle, until it gave way suddenly beneath me, flinging me forward into a patch of briars that thrust out from the hillside in an uncanny pattern, seeming to harbor some treacherous form of life.

Pain surged through me. Faintly, I heard someone scream. Had it been myself crying out in an agony of fear and pain? Or had it been the eerie wail of a marauding coyote chasing rabbits farther up the slope?

I lay stunned, listening.

A voice came to me from the heart of the dark thicket. It seemed very near and I lay paralyzed, the thorny stems prickling beneath me. Again the eerie whisper came, seeming to issue from the depths of the mountain, and I thought, as it persisted: I am going mad.

There was no need for me to strain to catch the hoarsely uttered words. I knew the message by heart.

"Don't remember, Cameo," it said. "If you do, something terrible will happen."

Suddenly I was clawing my way through the thicket, following insanely after that elusive, cruel sound. A pit yawned before me, a fathomless mouth opened to devour me. I reached for the gnarled bole of a manzanita and clung to it as the world dipped beneath me, a familiar and merciful haze blotting my mind.

I floated dreamily on the gentle wisps of fog. Someone spoke softly, out of the billowing gray haze, a voice from my past. It was a man's voice, telling me stories.

"Before the 1906 tremor, the slopes were hon-

eycombed with caves," the voice said. "There might very well yet be a hidden entrance behind any clump of wild lilac or sycamore, where ancient vintages sleep, great wines still drinkable after a hundred years because they were grown on the best of the great nineteenth-century vines. The root stock came from France before phylloxera destroyed the best of them. It is believed even now that there are thousands of cases of those rare wines yet to be exhumed from behind sealed openings. Their presence is an old myth here in our wine-growing country."

The fog grew thin, something harsh, frightening dissipating it, blotting out that gentle voice from my past. The ugly whisper again. . . .

"Don't remember, Cameo."

It was *real*, I thought, with a sudden surety, knowing that I had unwittingly stumbled onto one of the legendary cellars that someone had told me tales of long ago.

Whoever was stalking me was hidden there now, I thought, crouching beyond the black, yawning mouth in some horrendous dark cavern.

I scrambled to my feet, and ignoring the pain glancing along my leg, I half-ran, half-stumbled toward the comparative safety of the old house looming out of its black coppice of trees.

Chapter Thirteen

There were telltale scratches on my legs the following morning from my mad scramble along the slope. Nate noticed them when he appeared unexpectedly for breakfast.

"You've taken a fall on that weak ankle," he stated. "You should be more careful."

I searched his face warily, torn by ambivalence. "I went walking up the hill," I said cautiously.

"You shouldn't have. There's a good deal of poison oak up there. A skirmish with those poisonous vines could leave you broken out all over in ugly blisters." Yellow darts flicked through his eyes, seeming to warn me of some far greater danger than a few scraggly, reddened vines could ever pose.

"Maybe I am not susceptible," I said defensively.

"Not susceptible to what, Cammy?" Jefferey had appeared with Sabrina trailing closely behind him.

"Don't tell me that you consider yourself immune to Nate's charms, darling," Sabrina quipped, her black eyes growing avaricious as they lighted on Nate. "Or to Jefferey's either, for that matter. I find them both irresistible." She gave a knowing laugh.

"Until after the reading, at any rate," Jefferey commented, taking his place at the head of the table.

As usual, it was Nate who dominated the room, his immense vitality disturbing the otherwise static somberness of the old house.

Claudia came in from the direction of the kitchen, looking harassed. Jefferey arose and went around the table to give her a quick kiss as he seated her. Nate's "Good morning, Claudia," seemed lost on the small woman as she looked up almost despairingly into her eldest son's face.

"Darling, the most dreadful thing seems to have happened," she said.

Nate half-arose in his chair. "What is it, Claudia?" His voice sounded alarmed.

She flashed him an accusing look. "Maria. She didn't come in last night."

"Is that all." Nate slipped back into his chair.

"Jefferey?" A pleading look had come into Claudia's eyes.

"It's all right, Mother," Jefferey said. "Nate's lack of concern convinces me that all must be well with Maria."

"And just what is that meant to imply?" Nate demanded of his brother.

"Only that you no doubt know exactly where

154

Maria is at this precise moment. I won't elaborate in mixed company. It is enough to know that our little chili pepper is safe." Jefferey gave a wicked laugh.

Unexpectedly I recalled the scream I had half-heard the night before, as I lay wrapped in agony on the brink of the slope. I found myself concentrating desperately in an effort to draw a distinct line between the real and the unreal. Could it possibly have been Maria I had heard? Or had it been my own voice crying out? Or merely a coyote, as I had imagined at the time?

My thoughts grew confused and I turned my attention to Claudia, who was saying, "Have you seen her?" She searched Nate's face with her green eyes.

He said shortly, "We'll discuss it later."

"I should hope so, darling," Sabrina quipped.

An uneasy silence fell between us then and Nate finished his meal hurriedly, as though to escape the suspicion that had been cast on him. As he strode out of the dining room, I noticed that he had barely touched the steaming platter of food that Carmelita had set before him.

Later that same morning I wandered aimlessly out into the bright sunlight, watching the last vestiges of fog glide off of the ridges where it had lain throughout the night in a dense fleece. And found myself drifting up the slope away from the vines, toward the dark clump of brush that concealed the entrance to the hidden cellar.

Was Maria there somewhere inside the looming mountain? I wondered. Was she awaiting Nate in some secure trysting place? Or had some terrible fate befallen her, as the scream—if it had been real—would seem to indicate? Had Nate harmed her because of her recent attraction to Jesus Estralado? That he was a man who would be jealous of his women, I was certain.

Softly, I called Maria's name. My voice fell emptily on the languorous fall air. I paused to scan the vineyard below, wondering if I dared to slip into the hidden cellar by daylight to search for the missing girl, a shiver of fear going through me as I recalled the hoarse, threatening whisper.

Again the feeling of being watched came over me. I turned in a circle, searching, and saw Nate hurrying toward me from the direction of the winery.

"Dammit, Cammy," he said, when he had reached me. "I told you not to come up here." He took my arm and turned me roughly about, heading me away from the clump of brambles that hid the cellar's entrance.

I went with him warily. "I told you I am not susceptible to your poisonous vines," I said.

"I am susceptible if you aren't," he said. His voice was muffled suddenly to a quick, seething tenderness. "And I am not referring to poisonous vines."

Something so blindingly intimate moved behind his eyes that I caught my breath. What manner of man was this, I thought numbly, that he could be so fiercely independent one minute, so unbearably yielding the next?

"I don't know what you are getting at," I said.

"I thought you understood." He seemed suddenly angry with me, half-dragging me in the direction of the winery.

"I understand that you don't want me to know who I really am," I accused, dismayed by his sudden change of mood, thinking that I shouldn't be, that I should have realized by now that he was not an ordinary man, just as Jefferey had said.

He reached suddenly for my hand, squeezing it until it ached. "I don't give a damn who you are," he said. "I only want to look after you. Remember that."

We walked in silence, our feet releasing powdery little puffs of dust from the earth's dew-moistened crust. I should tell him about the scream, I thought. Instead, I said, "About Maria. . . Are you certain she's all right?"

He shot me a piercing look. "I've talked to the help. It happens that one of the pickers is absent this morning."

"Jesus Estralado?"

Nate nodded. "Sebastian is aware of what has been going on if Carmelita isn't. Like any mother, she prefers to think of her daughter as blameless."

"What if Maria doesn't come back?"

"There is no reason why she shouldn't."

157

"I hope you are right," I said, still thinking uneasily of the scream.

The sense of uneasiness stayed with me for the remainder of the day. By nightfall it had become imperative that I search the hidden cellar. I awaited my opportunity craftily.

Jefferey and Sabrina sat at a card table in Vinecroft's darkly paneled living room, Sabrina's voice cuttingly accusing Jefferey of not paying attention to the game they were playing. Claudia had curled herself into a corner of the large, brown velvet sofa with a magazine which apparently didn't interest her, while I tried to read one of the drab books I had brought in from the library, finding it impossible to concentrate in my present state of apprehensive determination.

Outside a car's engine roared to life, sending an inexplicable little shiver through me.

"Don't tell me Nate is actually tearing himself away from his precious vintage," Sabrina commented.

"He's going to look for Maria," Claudia said. "Jefferey insisted that he make some effort."

"Only because you have made such an issue of her absence," Jefferey interrupted her. "I can't imagine why you're so concerned."

"Do you think I haven't been aware of what has been going on?" Claudia snapped, seeming, for once, to be angry with her favored, older son. "I'm not blind, you know. I've seen."

"Please, Mother. Spare us the unsavory details," said Jefferey. There was a harsh note in his voice. His stormy eyes seemed to flash his mother some grim warning.

"Come, darling." Sabrina laid a pacifying hand on Jefferey's arm. "I find offhand references to Nate's peccadillos depressing, to say the least. Amuse me." The last words were a command.

Surprisingly, Jefferey turned his attention to their game without first making one of his pointed observations concerning Sabrina's motives for coming to Vinecroft.

It was only after the others had retired and the old house was shrouded in darkness that I dared to creep out into the moon-dappled night. The eucalyptus rustled restlessly above me as I slipped away from the gloomy mansion, their saber leaves turned to cut the sun even in darkness.

Unmindful of the dull ache in my ankle, I darted through the dense shadows, making my way warily past the winery. I told myself that Nate's absence from the grape farm seemed to have been arranged by a cooperative fate. Yet even as the dramatic thought entered my mind, I caught the powerful hum of the Mercedes.

As the car's headlamps came into view on the circling drive, I crouched furtively behind a clump of wild lilac, determined to carry out my search of the hidden cellar in spite of Nate's mercurial presence.

A moment later a car door slammed and I saw a

light flick on in the second story of the big house. Glimpsing Nate moving about beyond the out-dated lace curtains, I turned quickly and made my way up the slope, gliding stealthily from one black patch of shadow to the next.

The entrance to the secret cellar had been carefully obscured by a lacing of dry grass and twigs heaped to resemble a wood rat's nest. I plunged into the thicket, pulling the tangle free, heedless of the brambles that tore at my hands.

My light, when I flashed it through the yawning entrance, revealed a makeshift ladder. I glanced once more toward the house. Nate's light was no longer burning. Convinced that he had retired for the night and that I would be free to make my furtive search in comparative safety, I scrambled bravely down the wobbly steps.

The peculiar odor of dry rot reached to envelop me. I had smelled that strange aroma before under circumstances that escaped me. A passageway littered with fallen stone and cooperage long since fallen to kindling wood led away from me into the depths of the mountain. I followed it determinedly, softly calling Maria's name.

There was no reply. Nothing but the sound of my own voice echoing eerily along the cracked, stone walls. Vaulted caves opened off the main passageway at regular intervals. The smell of mold and decay was all around me, coupled with a virulent smell of wildlife. Bats, I thought, as one of the frightening little creatures dipped past me.

I made my way cautiously, following a path of sorts that had been worn into the dusty floor. It meandered crazily through the bewildering maze, first to the right then to the left. I tried not to think that I could very well become lost as I ventured deeper into the eerie, underground beehive.

A man's shoe print was visible from time to time in the deep accumulation of dust that had silted down onto the floor, and I found myself wondering what would happen if Nate should catch me here. What had he meant when he said that he wanted to take care of me? Had there been some unspeakable innuendo behind his words? Would I disappear suddenly as Gain Bantry had? And now Maria...?

The chilling questions teemed through my mind and I had the sudden feeling that I wasn't alone in the cellar, that I had been followed. I forced myself to hurry deeper into the cave, my light reflecting suddenly in something green and shiny. For a terrifying instant I fancied that I had ventured into the lair of some wild animal and that the green reflections came from slitted eyes watching me warily. I played the narrow beam wildly, my heart pounding. Then saw that it was only a bottle that had caught the ribbon of light, casting it back at me, and that there were a great many of them racked ahead of me along the narrow passageway, their slender necks wrapped in tarnished leadfoil.

Someone had disturbed the layers of cobwebs and dust that must once have blanketed them. Nate, I thought, attempting to determine their worth, thinking too that he had borrowed money recklessly when he need only to exhume the fortune in rare vintage that lay before me to redeem himself.

Everything about Nate Bantry suddenly seemed to fall into place as I played my light along the dusty racks. His precocious adventures as a child—it must have been then that he had stumbled onto the hidden cellar; his determined efforts to maintain Vinecroft after Gain Bantry had disappeared; his confident assurance that Bantry wines would come into their own again as gold medal winners. And soon, I couldn't help thinking, as I recalled the excitement that had seethed in his eyes.

I had the uncanny feeling that Nate had taken fate into his own hands. It was a frightening thought and I moved uneasily along the passageway, glimpsing the harvest dates printed on the yellowed labels. Bottles of the great nineteenth-century years, I thought, reading the unbelievable numerals. 1870. 1893. 1895. Then wondered how I had known which vintages had been rare. Had Gain Bantry—my father—once told me? Had he known of this secret cache? Was it to be a part of his eagerly anticipated legacy? It occurred to me suddenly that as Gain Bantry's daughter I might very well be included in his will.

162

Relentlessly, a new barrage of questions invaded my mind. Had Gain—my father—somehow indicated to me before he vanished that I was someday to inherit a share of his precious grape farm? Furthermore, had he confided his intention to Nate? Was that why Nate insisted so vehemently that I hold memory at bay?

I pushed deeper into the tunnel, the incredible thoughts numbing me, blotting out the reality of the musty cave with its fortune in vintage.

Chapter Fourteen

I came onto yet another precious cache, this one containing racks of champagne, the thick, dark magnums carefully tilted to dampen the corks. Someone had constructed a desk of sorts nearby, from an odd assortment of boxes. There were several metal containers tucked into the various cubbyholes. Curious, I opened one of them.

The box contained several spiral notebooks, their pages filled with a painstaking tally of the innumerable bottles racked in the hidden cellar, listing the names of the wines and their harvest dates.

A second box held an assortment of papers and clippings. I leafed through them, the word CAMEO BABY blazing up at me from their midst. My hands trembled as I withdrew the yellowed newspaper clipping, scanning the impersonal, gray print. Just as Benita Emery had hoped, in her letter to Gain, her child had been taken to a home for foundlings. If the child's parents couldn't be located, the article said, the infant would in all probability be put out eventually for adoption.

I found it difficult to associate the impersonal words with myself. Yet I knew that I had been that child.

A legal document tucked among the sheaf of papers caught my eye. As I unfolded the long, stiff pages, the name *Cameo* again sprang out at me. *I hereby bequeath one half of my worldly possessions to one Cameo Considine....*

Stunned, I realized that I held a copy of Gain Bantry's will. Cameo Considine? But I was Cameo Corwin, I thought numbly. What did it mean? Had Nate, in his eagerness to locate Gain's daughter, mistaken me for someone else? Who was I, I thought crazily. Why couldn't I remember?

A stealthy sound came to me from the depths of the cellar, interrupting my staggering thoughts. I stood paralyzed by a sudden, icy fear telling myself that it had been a pack rat scurrying about
164

among the sagging racks, even as some atavistic instinct told me that I wasn't alone.

Maria. Was she hidden somewhere in the intricate maze of tunnels? Or perhaps Gain. . . ?

I snapped off my light and pressed my back against the cold, stone wall between the racks, the sheaf of papers still clutched in my hand. An instant later, someone entered the passageway and came toward me, flashing a light over the dusty rows of bottles. Whoever it was reached to remove one of them and as his head came into the sphere of light I saw that he was masked.

Nate, I thought numbly, evaluating his hidden fortune. His progress toward me was leisurely. I thought how chillingly cruel he was, how deliberately cold-blooded; certain that he must have glimpsed me from his window and followed me up the slope; that he must know that I cowered now in quaking terror mere inches from him.

Then suddenly a woman's voice pierced the black silence, echoing angrily through the rockbound maze. "You are mad! Caging me here like a wild animal!" It was Maria's voice, and I thought stupidly: She is still alive, then.

But for how long? The icy thought struck me as I grasped the meaning of her words. Caged. I could no longer deny that there was a madman roaming about Vinecroft.

The masked figure had turned and was hurrying back the way he had come. Deliberately, I refused to give him a name as I made a cautious movement forward, knowing that I must somehow find my way out of the cellar and go for help. Jefferey, I thought. I must bring Jefferey before it was too late.

I inched my way slowly along the passage, my hand groping along the racks that sagged dangerously beneath their precious load. Sickeningly, my toe caught against a protruding brace and I clawed blindly at the rotting wood, hearing it crackle beneath my touch, the small sounds ringing like pistol shots through the icy darkness.

I realized that the rack was slowly beginning to collapse and I lurched away from it as a bottle crashed to the floor, the sheaf of papers I still carried flying from my hand. Miraculously, I still had my light. Snapping it on, I ran ahead of the seeping dark pool that reflected its beam like blood.

Somehow I found the secret opening and climbed the ladder quickly, not looking back, aware of footsteps pounding toward me through the hollow, stone corridors. The vines shadowing the slope below me seemed to offer sanctuary from that dark, pursuing form and ignoring the screaming pain in my ankle, I fled into them to crouch in terror beneath the sulfurous fronds.

He came running down the slope after me and I stopped breathing, thinking that he would surely hear the desperate pounding of my heart. Pain glanced through me in lightning flashes and I knew, although I hadn't been conscious of it at the time, that I had given my ankle a vicious turn on the wobbly ladder. It would have been impossible for me to run from him had I wanted to. My only hope was to stay hidden beneath the vine until he had gone.

Or until he ferreted me out like a wounded rabbit.

He came nearer. I could see his masked form through the broad leaves, pausing mere feet from me to listen. Then, after a paralyzing eon, miraculously leaving, striking off up the slope, his footsteps muffled by the thick, brown dust between the rows.

I closed my eyes and waited, the pain in my ankle gradually subsiding into a mere throb. It seemed another eternity before I dared at last to creep out of hiding. The mountain crested ominously above me, its slope meshed in a confusion of shadows. I studied them warily, moving slowly along the row.

Then suddenly something moved. Someone. And I knew that I had been tricked. He was still there, waiting in the black pool beneath the live oaks. He moved almost casually out of the shadows, walking toward the mansion, cutting me off from its looming safety.

Ignoring the throb in my ankle, I bolted between the vines. I was halfway across the vineyard before I dared to glance back over my shoulder. He stood in a patch of moonlight making no effort to follow me. I had the fantastic thought that he wasn't real, that the night was playing some cruel trick on me.

Or was it my mind inventing frightening fantasies to fill the fathomless, gray void that should have been filled with memories?

Then he moved, throwing aside the screened mask, striding purposefully toward the house that jutted forlornly out of the trees. I stared after him wondering what mad turn his thoughts had taken that he should suddenly ignore my fleeing presence. I sensed a deadliness about him that made him seem more ominous than ever and I plunged on between the vines driven by a fear more chilling than any I had ever known.

Frantically, I tried to devise a plan. I would make my way somehow to St. Felicia, I decided. Go to Gain Bantry's lawyer. Lockridge. Yes, that had been the name. Thank God I had remembered. Perhaps he could help me, send help to Maria.

I had come to the edge of the vineyard. The drive curved away from it, a silver ribbon undulating softly into black shadow. I stumbled onto it unaware of the small, darkly insidious vine that spread deadly tentacles into the velvet dust until it twined prickly fingers around my aching ankle and flung me down with fearful suddenness. Pain washed through me in waves, swirling, swelling, sweeping me backward in time to relive a forgotten nightmare.

A car surged toward me unswerving, somehow

black and evil. Memory carried its sound with jarring clarity, what had begun as a far-off angry purr building to an ear-shattering roar. The sound vibrated through me, accompanied by a dazzling wash of light.

Then I realized that this was no ordinary nightmare. The car plummeting toward me was real. I crouched in the glare of its headlights for a blinding instant, knowing that I had lived this moment before in another time, another place.

It was purely reflex that sent me rolling into the ditch beside the narrow drive, imbuing my rubbery arms and legs with a surging strength that carried me deep among the vines.

I burrowed beneath the broad, rough leaves, memory swelling in my mind like white-hot fire.

There was another vineyard mantling dusty, red slopes. Zinfandels, invading a Spanish style courtyard. . . . A woman sitting in their shadow, all but hidden by the festoons of royal green leaves. . . .

Memory dissolved the shadows around me, illuminating her face. My mother, Mary Considine. A man appeared beside her. There was a certain magic in his eyes and I knew that he was my father even before memory gave him a name. John. John Considine. He had been a vintner. I saw myself, Cameo Considine, a wide-eyed child happily listening to his tales of the vines as I followed him about the vineyards, absorbing the magic and wonder of it all.

Eventually, I had gone away to business school. It was something my mother and I had dreamed of and planned for. Still I had been torn when the minute came to part from them. Perhaps I'd had a premonition, for I never saw either of them again. . . .

Memory became knife-edged, slashing the gray curtain mercilessly. There was a stranger telling me my father was dead. There had been an accident. My mother was still alive, he said. She lived long enough to tell me about the brooch hidden in her jewelry case. A cameo. . . .

Then she was gone, too, and I was alone. Alone with the strange story she had whispered to me during those last terrible moments of her life. Alone beneath the vines mantling the courtyard. Alone inside the ancient winery and the cellars where I still imagined I heard his footsteps, my father not dead after all but moving through the shadows attending his wines. Alone and wondering and knowing that I would go mad if I didn't get away. . . .

I was packing that first time I saw the car, a black Mercedes, not new but gleaming with wax. I saw it again as my bus pulled out for San Francisco and a third time outside my apartment, waiting. . . .

Memory washed over me in waves and I saw myself running, the ungodly screech of rubber ringing in my ears. The sound of a man's voice calling my name, boldly now, no longer bothering with disguise. . . .

No longer a memory. I pushed deeper beneath the vine.

"Cammy! I know you're there." He had come nearer.

I held my breath, wondering how I had escaped him that night on Telegraph Hill. What horror lay beyond the scope of my memory? Had I somehow thrown myself out of the path of his plunging car? Nate's car, I thought. Jefferey's cast-off.

"Cammy! Come out, for God's sake. It's Jefferey, darling. I'm not going to harm you."

Jefferey. I stirred beneath the vines, dismayed by the similarity between his voice and Nate's. Did I dare to believe that it actually was Jefferey attempting to lure me out of hiding? Or was it Nate being clever again?

"Cammy! Must I come searching for you. You know how I loathe these smelly vines. Sulfurous things! Why Nate insists on smelling the whole place up with his vile farmer's concoctions I shall never understand." The note of distaste in his voice sounded genuine.

I crawled from beneath the thick leaves, those that had fallen crackling beneath my hands.

"Nate," I said. "I thought it was Nate. He tried to kill me."

"*Nate* tried to kill you?" Jefferey seemed stunned. Then suddenly his laughter rang out, renting the soft silence of the night. "Forgive me,

171

darling. I had to do that. Relief. Do you realize that *I* came close to running you down just now? What in God's name were you doing here, crouched in the road like that?" He drew a violent breath. "*I* might have killed you."

"Nate," I repeated. "I have to get away. Get into town. He's stalking me. He has put Maria in a cage." My voice rose, and I swallowed to bring it under control.

"Darling, for God's sake!" I felt Jefferey's arm go around me, smelled the sweetness of his cologne and that other illusive odor that sometimes clung to him, not actually aware of either one as I yielded to his comforting manner. "Perhaps you will believe me now when I tell you that my brother is utterly mad."

"Please help me," I said.

"You're frightened, and no wonder." Jefferey's voice was soft and soothing. Nate's voice, I thought again, adding a stinging piquancy to the moment.

He guided me toward the car that was parked a short distance down the drive. It occurred to me to ask him where he had been going at this late hour.

"Into town to search for Maria," he said. "Nate came back without her. Now I understand why, if what you said is true. My God, darling. I really don't understand."

"She's in the cellar. A hidden cellar on the

brink of the slope. We have to reach her before it's too late."

Jefferey helped me into the car without comment and went around to slide beneath the wheel. The engine roared to life and he turned the Mercedes about, his face grim in the faint glow of the dashlights.

"I'm afraid," I said with a little shiver.

"It's all right. I'll look after you. See that you are kept safe. Obviously something has to be done about Nate. If, as you say, he has locked Maria up in some dark cavern, as his brother it is up to me to see that he is taken care of. He was always Gain's golden boy but little good it will do him after this." A glib satisfaction had come into his voice and I thought how much he hated Nate.

There was more than male rivalry between the two of them. Something unspeakable, I thought with a shudder, wondering why I was still afraid.

I heard myself saying defensively, "Nate has been under a terrible strain. Working so hard to keep the farm going all of these years. Striving to support Claudia, and Sabrina while she has been between husbands. And you," I added, unable to hold the words back.

Jefferey stiffened beside me. "You are still attracted to him in spite of everything," he accused. "Even Sabrina isn't immune to his questionable charms. But then I'm not surprised. History is filled with women who were attracted to madness."

I made a small sound of protest.

"It's quite all right, Cammy. I forgive you your infatuation with my brother," Jefferey said.

"What are you going to do?" I asked.

"Subdue him, of course. An institution, perhaps. It seems to be the only answer. I suppose you've some idea why he tried to kill you."

We had come into the shadow of the winery. Jefferey cut the car's engine and leaned toward me, his profile dark against the soft gleam of the windshield. A subtle sense of wariness came over me.

"I had something he wanted," I said.

"That ridiculous brooch, perhaps," Jefferey said.

"Brooch?"

"The cameo. I notice that you no longer wear it."

But I hadn't worn it since my arrival at Vinecroft. The thought seeped slowly into my mind, became suddenly electric. How could Jefferey have known about it, then? I wondered wildly. How?

I became suddenly aware of the peculiar odor that clung to him, mingling with the rich scent of his cologne. It was the unmistakable smell of dry rot and decay.

Chapter Fifteen

I moved sharply away from him.

"I shouldn't have mentioned the brooch," Jefferey said softly.

He made no move to restrain me. There was only the weight of his hand resting lightly on my shoulder, its touch grazing my flesh with an icy chill.

"And all the while I thought it was Nate," I said in a numb voice.

I noticed now that Jefferey wore jeans and a faded work shirt. Nate's clothes hugging his body, giving him that trim, lithe appearance. . . .

"I intended that you should," he said.

"I remember now. The car that followed me to San Francisco was polished. Sabrina said that you like spit and polish, while Nate. . . ."

"You have remembered far too much," Jefferey said. "In spite of my efforts to warn you. It wasn't easy slipping about, watching your every move."

"I don't suppose it was." I wondered that I could speak so calmly, even as my mind busily calculated the distance down the path to the house.

Had I a chance, I wondered. My breath quickened. In a single, lunging movement, I threw open the car door, tumbling out onto the ground. Jefferey plunged after me. I screamed as he pinned me beneath him, the sound gurgling in my throat as his hand came around to cover my mouth.

"You shouldn't have done that, Cameo," he breathed into my ear.

Below us a light flared in an upper window of the old house. Briefly I glimpsed a woman's slender form silhouetted against it.

Then Jefferey was pulling me roughly into the uncertain shadows of the eucalyptus, keeping his hand firmly planted over my mouth as he half dragged, half-carried me through the tangled growth above the vineyard.

We came at last to the entrance of the hidden cellar and I struggled against him as I felt myself being drawn downward into the depths of the mountain. His free hand slashed angrily across my cheek, moving to produce a flashlight from somewhere. I felt it press into my back as he dragged me along the musty tunnel.

The cold beam of light danced haphazardly over the dusty racks, casting black witch's shadows on the walls. The cellars seemed to ramble endlessly. After what seemed an eternity of rock bound twistings and turnings, Maria's voice came suddenly out of the darkness ahead, echoing weirdly.

"Jefferey? Is that you?" She sounded both angry and frightened.

Her cry seemed to come from one of the great, oval casks racked in this section of the underground maze, their staves gray with age, their bands rusted and peeling. I remembered the legend and gave a gasp of horror.

"It's quite all right, Cammy," Jefferey said. "You may scream now, if you'd like. No one at the house can possibly hear you."

"You're mad!" I said.

I had the sensation that none of it was real: the girl inside the cask; Jefferey striking a match, reaching to touch it to the charred wick of a candle cemented in wax to the top of one of the crumbling casks.

"Perhaps," Jefferey remarked calmly, when he had blown out the match.

"What are you going to do with us?" I asked.

"Kill you, of course." The winning smile that had become so familiar to me sat incongruously on his mouth. "I've a crypt for you as well."

Inside the cask Maria gave a strangled cry.

"That should come as no surprise to you, my little chili pepper," Jefferey said, rapping against the carved head that was checked with age and held in place by several well-nailed planks. "You've become far too clever for your own good. Your impromptu story of a *fantasma* convinced me of that. It wasn't enough that Vinecroft has a legend. You had to elaborate."

177

This is the first I've heard of it, Nate had told me.

"Maria made up the ghost," I said. "Her Spirit of the Cask."

"Her motives were purely selfish. She wanted to frighten you away, in case you haven't already guessed. Naturally, once she had told you that wild tale, I tried to smooth it over."

"Después de mucho hablarme, me pintó un violín!" In her hour of terror, Maria had resorted to an inborn language. *After a lot of talk, he didn't keep his word....*

I looked at Jefferey.

"The little bitch imagined that I was going to marry her." He gave a cruel laugh. "Sebastian and his insane tales of yesteryear! He managed to convince Maria that she should be mistress of Vinecroft, simply because that first Bantry's unfortunate sister-brides happened to be Revis-Geraras. Since they both died and as a consequence Maria wasn't born to the privilege, she decided that she must marry into it. The meanderings of a twisted mind!" Ironically, Jefferey shook his head, giving another of his mad laughs. "She has been after Nate for years, the two of them slipping around. Then one night the little bitch managed to follow me here. And once she realized what I'd found in the heart of this mountain, she became more than eager to exchange her hot little body for a share. Naturally it was necessary for me to make a few rash promises to keep

178

her quiet about all of this. Then you came along, Cammy darling, and diverted both my own attention and Nate's. Maria saw you as a threat to her hoped-for security and made up her ghost, expecting you to run like a scared rabbit."

"You fool!" Maria's voice echoed out of the cask. "It was because she could view the hillside from the library windows that I invented the *fantasma*. Even yet you fail to understand that she might easily have seen you coming here. I invented the ghost to protect you!"

"Really, Maria," Jefferey said. "You could hardly expect a bright girl like Cammy to mistake me for a female ghost. Better to let her imagine that I was Nate, one reason I've resorted to wearing his smelly farmer's garb for our little rendezvous. Not that I've been fool enough to imagine that I am the only one sharing your dubious favors." His voice was suddenly derisive. Sneering. "I haven't forgotten that it was Nate you chased after first. Are still chasing after. Just as Gain preferred him over me—" He broke off and this time his laughter was brittle with hatred.

He gave me a leering smile, the flickering candlelight playing over his handsome face, illuminating his strange, green eyes so that they shimmered like polished stones.

"Gain's daughter," he said then. "Even so, you'd have made a beautiful chatelaine."

There was a dark look of madness about him that set cold fingers clutching urgently at my heart.

Time, I thought. I need time. Perhaps my scream
had been heard at the house. Perhaps that was
why the light had flicked on. Perhaps someone
would come. If only I can keep him talking, I
thought desperately.

I said, "Gain Bantry.... My father. Do you
know what happened to him?"

Again that mad, cruel laugh. "If there are such
things as ghosts, Vinecroft is now blessed with
two Spirits of the Cask wandering about over
these ugly slopes. Let us hope they enjoy each
other's company."

My eyes were drawn against my will to the rank
of ancient casks lining the passage walls. "No!" I
whispered. "No!"

"Nate was his golden boy," Jefferey said. "I
hated them both for that. It was while I was searching for Nate one day that I found this cellar
long before Gain married Claudia and the three
of us came to live here. I knew even then that it
was only a matter of time before both Gain and
Nate must die. I didn't realize, of course, that
Gain had a daughter. He had guarded his secret
well. It wasn't until I had . . . taken care of Gain
and found the evidence in his safe, that I knew.
Everyone assumed that he had taken his valuable
papers with him. While the truth was, I had spied
on him, knew where he kept the keys. There was
a copy of his will and the clipping referring to
Cameo Baby. You, Cammy darling. He'd kept
close tabs on your precious little life, written
180

all down for some reason, kept a diary of sorts. He knew exactly where you were all those years, had watched you grow. . . ."

"But he never—"

"He was very stealthy about it, darling. Little periodic jaunts away from Vinecroft to confer with other vintners in the state. Considine Winery was on his itinerary. No doubt he used an assumed name when he called on your adoptive father, just to be on the safe side. To protect you perhaps, since it would hardly have been to your best interests to have it become known that you were his bastard."

I flinched, the words Jefferey had uttered overwhelming me. A jumble of images cluttered my mind, the sun-browned faces of the vintners who had appeared from time to time to confer with the man I had imagined to be my father. Which of those intent men had been Gain Bantry—my real father? The question was too shattering to cope with.

I forced it from my mind.

"You came there after my parents were killed," I said. "It was you watching the house through binoculars. Following me to San Francisco, in Nate's Mercedes."

"Watching you, darling. I read of your adoptive parents' death in the paper. Knew that you were alone, that it would be a simple matter to be rid of you. Fate seemed to be working in my favor."

I shivered. "You tried to run me down in San

Francisco." But what had happened then, I won‐
dered. Why couldn't I complete the memory?

"And imagined that I had succeeded," Jeffere‐
was saying. "You can imagine my shock when
read in the paper that you had been found *alive*
The Cameo Girl. I was watching for a story. Bu
not that particular one."

"They said I was found on the cliffs below For
Ross." I had a sudden thought. "You must hav‐
driven there with my . . . body, after you ran m‐
down. Dumped me over, thinking that I was al‐
ready dead. It had to be something like that
Then you went back to San Francisco and burned
the apartment house."

"You are very clever, darling. But not nearl‐
clever enough. You should have known bette
than to regain your memory. I tried to war‐
you."

"Nate's car. . . . It was damaged when yo‐
struck me. There was evidence—"

"Hardly. You see, darling, I simply bashed i
into a tree on my way back here in the wee hour‐
Stumbled into the house inebriated. Naturall
Nate was disgusted, but of course he could hav
hardly guessed the real story behind that battere
grill. Oh, I am fully as clever as you are, Camm‐
I even thought to run my own car over a scatte
ing of nails that had somehow got spilled on th
driveway. It gave me an excuse to take Nate's ca
that weekend. Sabrina had invited me to one ‐
her parties. I dropped in on her but only lon

enough for her to say that I had been there. You see, I thought of everything."

"But how did you know I would be leaving the Cholami Hills? Coming to San Francisco?"

"Fate, darling. Purely fate. Imagine my delight when I saw you stepping onto the bus in Cholami City, your gear all packed. Before, I had intended to make it look like suicide, a girl alone in that rambling, stucco house, depressed over the loss of both parents. When Gain's will was read you'd simply have been deceased."

"It must have come as a shock to you to discover that Nate had taken me under his wing," I said.

"That is the one thing that continues to puzzle me. Nate was always left behind when Gain made his circuit of the wineries, most particularly the Considine Winery located in the Cholami Hills. I was certain Gain had kept the secret of your exisence from him."

"There was a letter in one of the formularies," I said, "From my mother."

"Your mother?"

"My real mother, Benita Emery. It stated her reasons for . . . abandoning me. She'd pinned the cameo brooch to my blanket to identify me for Gain."

"When the story about the Cameo Girl came out in the papers Nate must have realized who you were even though they misprinted the initials on the back of that damned brooch. At the time, it seemed another act of fate. Now I realize

183

that I should have ripped that damned doodad off your collar. Destroyed it." He was suddenly raving. "Killed the bastard who came snooping around bribing the old tales out of Sebastian for use in his gossipy book. Murdered Sabrina for presenting Nate with a copy of that defamatory work. Sued the damned publishers."

"It's a little late to do all of that," I said bravely, still vying for time. If anyone had heard my feeble scream and had somehow managed to trace Jefferey's progress with me along the slope, they should have been here by now, I thought despairingly. I would have to think of something. Do something. If only I could keep him talking. "Especially if you . . . harm Maria and me," I went on boldly. "One disappearance might not be too difficult to understand. But an entire rash of them? Be reasonable, Jefferey. You can't get away with it."

"*Can't* I, darling?" The chilling gleam had intensified in his eyes. "*Your* cask is ready, and another for my dear brother. Who will ever know since I will be the only one left who knows about this cellar? They can hardly prosecute anyone for murder without a corpus delicti. Not even that old bastard Lockridge, who insisted on a cour order to tie up Gain's property all these years Now, darling, I really am rather sorry. . . ." Jefferey turned away from me toward a cask that was different from the others; that, I saw, with surging sense of horror, had been pieced bac together. Repaired, just as the cask in which h

184

had caged Maria had been renovated against possible escape.

The cold fingers tightened around my heart. I wasn't ready to die. Vaguely, I glimpsed the arched mouth of yet another cellar a short distance down the passageway, and wondered how far I might get without a light. I had to try. My flight would divert Jefferey from Maria. Perhaps if I were lucky I could save us both.

I chose a moment when both Jefferey's hands were involved with the frightening head of the huge cask. He had laid his flashlight aside and there was only the feeble flickering of the candle driving back darkness. I leaned quickly toward it and blew. The darkness closed around us like a cold, black wall and I plunged into it, feeling for guidemarks, my fingers coming into contact at last with the splintery staves of a reeling cask.

"You damned little fool," Jefferey raged behind me.

I ran blindly and by some miracle found the opening off of the main passage that I had set as my goal. There were bottles racked here, my fumbling hands told me, and I raced recklessly between them, heedless of the darting pain in my ankle.

Somewhere behind me Jefferey cursed. He had found his flashlight and its cold beam found me, casting my shadow into the darkness ahead. Another black mouth yawned at my left and I swerved into it, my hands floating helplessly before me.

Then contacting something at last, the leadfoil-wrapped neck of a champagne magnum, and another. I ran on, my fingers brushing over them.

Then suddenly the floor of the cellar seemed to give way, for a shattering instant. When I found it again with my stumbling foot, the impact sent me reeling sideways into the laden rack. The aged wood groaned dangerously beneath my weight and I rolled away from it instinctively covering my face as I bumped over the downward jogs in the stone floor that had caused me to fall.

There was a violent explosion as one of the bottles rattled onto the floor. And another. It seemed then that the entire world exploded around me and I lay helplessly, my face buried in my arms, thinking that this was it. This was the end.

As quickly as it had begun, the holocaust subsided. I listened disbelievingly. There was no sound to indicate Jefferey's presence in the cellar. Yet he had been close behind me before the bottles exploded, I was certain of it. I had imagined even as I pressed my face into my arms that I had glimpsed his light turning the corner, had seen his dark form moving terrifyingly nearer.

Was he lying in wait for me, I wondered, anticipating the moment when I would betray myself with some slight movement so that he might pounce on me with the cruel skill of a cat toying with a mouse? I recalled his chilling laughter, telling myself that he was capable of just such a cunning maneuver.

186

I forced myself to lie quietly. The vivacious aroma of the wines rose around me, their misty moistness stinging my flesh where it had been grazed by the flying glass. I became aware of something warmly viscous seeping along my thigh. Whatever pain there might have been from the cut was absorbed by the jagged darts of pain shooting upward from my twisted ankle. The lightning flashes seemed uncannily to drive back the darkness.

Then I realized that someone was flashing a light along the passage from the end opposite the arched opening through which I had entered. Jefferey, I thought, winding through the beehive of tunnels to surprise me from behind.

I scrambled to my feet and lunged heedlessly through the hazardous debris, unmindful of the pain that enveloped me, knowing only that I must get away.

I didn't see Jefferey's body until I had stumbled against it. The light coming from behind me flashed over his face, illuminating, for a horrifying instant, the shard of green glass that protruded hideously from one sightless eye.

"Cammy!" someone said nearby.

I thought numbly: This time it has to be Nate.

A nightmare week followed and it was only Nate's indomitable presence that sustained us all. Jefferey was laid to rest. And Gain. . . .

The reading of the will was to take place in a

187

few days. I would be present as Cameo Considine. Nate had admitted to me that he had snatched the name "Corwin" out of the blue. The private investigator he had hired to trace my identity hadn't yet discovered my real name when Nate first appeared at General Hospital where I had been taken after the skin divers found me, to take me under his wing.

"It was the Cameo Girl story in the paper that set me off," Nate said now. The two of us were having coffee in Vinecroft's big kitchen, which seemed sunnier than the rest of the rambling old house. Or was it only because Nate was looking at me in that special way, something warm and eager burning behind his amber eyes? "In spite of the fact that the initials appearing on the back of the brooch had been misprinted," he continued. "I'd discovered Benita Emery's letter shortly after Gain disappeared. I suppose I knew then that someday our paths would have to cross. I called Cassidy the same day the Cameo Girl story appeared, and set the wheels in motion. I confided in Lockridge and got him to influence the superior court judge with some fancy, legal legerdemain to have my guardianship granted. It wasn't too difficult to do, since Lockridge and Gain had been close friends."

"And what if it had turned out that I wasn't Gain's daughter, after all your clever maneuvering?" I said.

"I knew you were someone special the minute

188

I laid eyes on you, lying so white and still in that big, impersonal ward. It was something in your face. Some part of Gain showing through. Or maybe it was just a feeling I had." He gave me a quick, endearing smile. "At any rate, I was determined to bring you to Vinecroft. Although I must confess that I had no real intention then of falling madly in love with you. I was doing it for Gain, in the beginning, out of gratitude and devotion. You were his daughter. . . . Then, without my quite realizing how it happened, there was suddenly something more to it than that."

"More to what, darling?" Sabrina stepped into the room, her pert face curious.

"You do pick your moments, don't you, Cousin?" Nate gave her a tolerant glance.

"Am I interrupting something?" Sabrina asked innocently. She poured coffee for herself and brought it to the table. "Poor Jefferey. I suppose you were discussing him. Incredible that none of us realized. . . . None of us except Claudia. I think she knew, or at least suspected, that something was wrong. It worried her that he was carrying on with Maria. She went so far as to mention that fact to me, hoping that I might somehow influence him. Perhaps I did." Sabrina drew a halting breath. "Maria can't stay on here, of course," she said then.

"Jesus plans to take her with him when he goes. Sebastian and Carmelita are agreeable. The two of them will be leaving as soon as the vintage

189

is in." Nate's gaze strayed to the ranks of vines beyond the tall windows.

"The keeper of the vine." Sabrina shot me a look, then glanced once more at Nate. "What about me? And Claudia? Now that we've some idea what is in that damned will. . . . Imagine Jefferey concealing those papers all this time just waiting, pretending all the while to have such a deathly fear of the cellars. I'd no idea he was so clever. Or you, Cammy." She gave a dismayed little laugh. "Turning up after all these years." Her dark gaze flashed to Nate. "Why did you find it so necessary to deceive us, darling? Attempting to pass Cammy off as your secretary. The whole thing is incredible to say the least."

"Suffice it to say that I knew what the reaction would be here at Vinecroft if I let you know that she was Gain's daughter. With the reading of his will in sight, your first thought would have been that she had arrived intending to contest it."

"But you deceived Cammy as well, darling."

"I was only trying to protect her from herself; give her an opportunity to grow strong again after the ordeal she had been through before I foisted too many cold facts onto her. You see, I actually believed she had attempted suicide and failed." He gave me a pleading look. "I realize now that I should have known better. But Cassidy had come up with the tragic story of your parents' deaths. I supposed it had been too much for you. The fact that your apartment house had burned that same
190

night seemed to be nothing more than a weird coincidence. The shorthand pin you were wearing gave me the idea to represent you as my secretary. I knew you needed strings attaching you to something, someone, lost as you were in your gray world. And so I forged an application for a job; tried to make it all seem logical."

"I suppose the incredible part of it is that you managed to bamboozle us. At least for awhile," Sabrina said.

"To me, the incredible thing is that I didn't catch on to what Jefferey had done. Was attempting to do," Nate said.

"It only goes to prove that you are human after all," Sabrina said. She turned to me. "Do you realize, darling, that you and I are actually cousins? I can't imagine why Gain denied you all those years, if he knew."

"That damned legend," Nate said. "Gain had some queer notions concerning the women in his life, as you very well know, Sabrina. I suppose Benita's pathetic letter seemed to him to bear them out, which explains why he didn't claim Cammy as an infant, why he was content to keep tabs on her incognito."

"My uncle was a good man for all of his eccentricities," Sabrina said. "Forgive me, Cammy. But perhaps he also took into account the fact that you were.... How does one put such a thing tactfully? At any rate, you are *legitimately* a Considine. I know that it must have been comforting

191

to him to know that you were faring well. The fact that you were being reared in the traditions of the vine must have pleased him." A clever look suddenly possessed her face. "I have just thought of something rather startling. You and Cammy are, in effect, brother and sister, Nate darling!"

"For God's sake, Sabrina!" Nate flashed her a dismayed look. "I was hoping no one would bring up that peculiar angle."

"You can't blame a girl for trying," Sabrina quipped.

"Essentially, nothing has changed," Nate said. "There will always be a Vinecroft and you shall always be welcome."

"You seemed damnably sure of that for someone who has turned out to be so innocent," Sabrina said.

"I had faith in Gain," Nate said simply. He turned to me, his face solemn. "Cammy. I think it is time you became legally a Bantry. Gain would have wanted that as much as I do."

Beyond the narrow windows the vines were suddenly illuminated, their turning leaves shining in the sun. I thought that I had never seen anything so beautiful, as Nate's arms closed protectively around me. His breath gently stirred my hair.

Behind us, Sabrina said softly, "The oracle has spoken." For once there was no undercurrent of mockery in her voice.